Death on The Dock

JACKIE SHARP

Book Cover by V.H Nicholson

Edits by The Word Emporium

First Edition 2024

ISBN Paperback: 978-1-0691755-0-2

ISBN Hardback: 978-1-9992578-9-7

Contents

Prologue

Sarah Cooper stood on the deck of the Commodore and waved at Fiona, the new Marina Manager. "Good morning," she called, smiling as Fiona waved back.

Her friends, Jewel and Joseph, had gone fishing in the Cosmos, but Sarah wanted to take it easy. It had been a very busy few weeks, what with the murders and whatnot, plus she'd finally got around to organising her new cabin and settling into the Commodore.

"Good morning," a voice said behind her.

Sarah turned to see a tall, young man with a pleasant smile carrying a crab trap.

"Do you mind if I drop this off the dock?" he asked. "I was told the crabs are excellent around here."

"They are," Sarah said. "My friend makes fabulous crab cakes. Go ahead."

The young man dropped his trap over the dock and fastened the line to a cleat. "I'll be back in a few hours," he said and left.

Sarah made coffee, fussed around the cabin, and then picked up the book she'd bought weeks ago when she'd first arrived. The pages were a bit crumpled, and Sarah remembered how it had gone flying into the water when she bumped into Commodore Hiscocks.

"Can't change the past," she said aloud and settled herself into a chair. A good read, that's what she needed.

Sarah woke with the book resting on her chest.

"Hello there."

She looked up to see the young man standing beside her boat. "Sorry to wake you," he said. "I'll just pull my trap if that's okay."

Sarah smiled. "You go right ahead."

She stood and stretched. What a lovely, lazy day.

She heard splashing as the young man pulled his trap. The sound reminded her of Joseph's delicious crab cakes. Time for a bite of lunch, she thought and turned to go into the cabin.

A terrified scream made Sarah stumble, her heart jumping into her mouth.

She ran to the side of her boat. The man was standing on the dock, looking at his trap.

"What's wrong?" Sarah called. "Are you hurt?"

The man pointed to the trap with a trembling hand.

"It's an arm," he croaked. "It's a human arm."

Chapter One

The September sun was just an orange smear on the horizon. A solitary figure of a man, walked along the water's edge, his bare feet sinking into the damp sand with each step. He wore pants rolled up to his knees. The high tide lapped at the shore, its gentle waves erasing any trace of his presence, as if nature itself sought to keep his secrets.

The beach was deserted, save for a single dog walker in the distance. This young woman, lost in the glow of her phone screen and ignoring the little dog pulling at the leash, barely acknowledged the man's existence as she passed by. It was as if he were a ghost, a specter from another time, unseen and unnoticed by the world around him.

Shell Bay, once a bustling hub of holidaymakers and sun-seekers, now lay silent and empty. The laughter and chatter of summer had faded, leaving behind the stillness of a fall morning. A wisp of mist hung low over the beach. The man reveled in the solitude, knowing that this morning walk would probably be the last one for a while, so he should savor the freedom while he still had the chance.

Sand oozed between his toes, and the chilly ocean waves engulfed his feet and legs up to his calves. Above him, was the cry of the gulls as they circled and swooped.

The man paused, his gaze fixed on the distant horizon where the sky and sea merged into an indistinguishable blur. His mind wandered, as it had countless times before, to the decision that had brought him to this moment. Doubts and uncertainties swirled within him, an endless dance of questions without answers. Was he truly ready for what lay ahead? Had he made the right choice?

But even as these thoughts occupied his mind, the man knew there was no turning back. He had to finish what he started. There would be collateral damage—there always was. But he couldn't be responsible for the choices that people had already made. A part of him knew he was merely creating justification for his actions—actions which would inevitably have consequences. But not for him, if he was careful.

The man took a deep breath and filled his lungs with the fresh sea air. Reluctantly, he turned away from the water's edge and made his way up the beach to a small promenade where he had left his belongings.

With methodical precision, he dried his feet, pulled on his socks, and slipped into his shoes. As he smoothed down the wrinkled fabric of his pant legs, he felt a strange sense of finality, as if he were closing one door and stepping through another. Then he neatly folded his towel and started to walk back to town.

The man checked his phone for the time. Nearly 7:30 am. The Bean Express would be open, he thought. Time to grab a coffee before I start my brand new life. With a renewed sense of purpose, the man quickened his pace, his mind already anticipating the rich aroma and comforting warmth of a freshly brewed cup of coffee.

Chapter Two.

Linda Jenkins stirred under her bedcovers. Something had woken her. A noise seemed to be coming from far away. A loud, persistent jangling sound. And then there was the smell. It was familiar, but Linda, groggy from sleep and the red wine she had the night before, was having trouble placing whatever had assaulted her senses. Was there a fire? Was it the sound of fire trucks? That thought jerked her out of her dream-like state, and she sat up, her heart pounding.

"Damn it," she said out loud as she reached over to smack her alarm clock.

There was no fire. Linda recognised the smell wafting in through her open bedroom window.

"Agnes!" she shouted as she swung her legs over the side of the bed. "I've told you before, don't smoke outside my bedroom window."

Agnes Crofton was Linda's landlady. She was nosy and completely shameless about it. She often skulked outside Linda's apartment, hoping to catch part of a conversation or phone call, which she could then embellish into juicy pieces of inaccurate gossip and spread to her vast, faceless network in Shell Bay. Agnes had been delighted to rent this little apartment to Detective Sergeant Linda Jenkins, newly arrived from Victoria Major Crimes. What better source of gossip than a disgraced police officer?

Linda groaned softly. The sound of her own voice made her wince. Why did she finish that last bottle of wine? It had been the perfect weekend, the first one she'd had off since she'd been assigned to the Shell Bay RCMP detachment as a Sergeant. Her best friend Joanna had come to visit, and they had spent two glorious days exploring the seaside town. As she'd watched Joanna's car leave the driveway, she'd been overcome by a wave of self-pity, which had only been exacerbated by the wine.

Linda sat on her bed and rubbed her head. She needed coffee—probably two mugs of the strongest black brew possible—and a shower before she started her shift. She wasn't looking forward to getting back to work and reality. Having Joanna visit had been wonderful, but it reminded Linda of how lonely she was living in Shell Bay.

"You're so lucky to live here," Joanna had said wistfully as she'd hugged Linda goodbye. "It's such a beautiful, peaceful place." Linda didn't entirely agree, but she grudgingly acknowledged that the small seaside town was growing on her. She'd hated Shell Bay when she first arrived. It wasn't her scene at all. The narrow high street was crammed with picturesque boutique shops that didn't open until ten in the morning, and despite the charming residential streets that lined the cliffs which overlooked the crescent-shaped bay, on closer inspection, it was clear that Shell Bay's heyday was in the past.

A few stores had permanent closing down signs in the windows. Paint was peeling on some of the municipal buildings, and the town had been completely overlooked by the usual big brand stores. There was only one coffee shop, The Bean Express, one pub, and until recently, absolutely no trendy restaurants or wine bars. Joanna hadn't noticed the shabbiness or the odd scrawl of graffiti; she'd just oohed and ahhed at the trinket shops and had dragged Linda for walks along the promenade and down narrow streets that Linda had never noticed. "Right then," Joanna declared early Saturday morning. "Let's explore the whole town."

Linda had pretended to moan about it, but she actually enjoyed seeing Shell Bay through her friend's eyes. Joanna had visited Shell Bay many times as a child, and she was able to relive her childhood holidays, even though Joanna had to admit Shell Bay had changed.

"Oh darn," Joanna had said after persuading Linda to walk the entire length of Main Street until they came to a gravel track. "The museum is closed."

It looked like the museum had been closed for decades. The wooden building was a patchwork of mottled grey and black, where the rot and mold had set in. The cedar shingles on the sagging roof looked only to be attached by clumps of moss. Weeds grew knee-high around the foot of the building, and the only indication that the building had once been the Shell Bay Museum was a faded sign that hung from one lone rusty nail above the entrance door, which was secured by a chain and a large padlock and bolt.

"Why would anyone bother chaining it?" Linda had wondered out loud, her police instincts trained to spot anything unusual. "Surely there can't be anything valuable in there?"

"What a shame," Joanna had said. "I remember visiting as a child. Why would the town let the Museum fall apart like this?"

Linda had shrugged, and they'd carried on with their weekend fun, although Linda had mentally filed the derelict building as a possible location for vandals and petty criminals.

It had been the only disappointment in the entire weekend. Joanna's enthusiasm had been infectious; even Agnes had been charmed by her.

"Oh well," Linda muttered to herself. "Back to reality."

Reality was probably a pile of paperwork on Linda's desk, which Constable Ray Reynolds found excuses to avoid over the weekend. There would be the usual complaints about noise from feuding neighbours, maybe a fight outside the pub, traffic violations, and if the weekend had been really busy, a shoplifting incident or two.

The main reason for Linda's dismay at her posting to Shell Bay was the lack of decent crime to solve. As Detective Inspector Linda Jenkins back in Victoria, she'd been used to high-speed chases after drug dealers or dangerous confrontations in murky industrial estates. There was nothing that Linda loved more than feeling the adrenaline pumping as she pulled on a stab vest and checked her standard-issue Smith & Wesson firearm before heading out to nab some bad guys. Linda's first impression of Shell Bay's criminal element was hugely disappointing. A few pimply youths who stole bicycles and an elderly gentleman who forgot to pay for his cigarettes were the highlight of Linda's first week. She was going to hate her posting in Shell Bay, she'd been sure. That might have also had something to do with being sent here as punishment and missing out on a promotion, which, in Linda's mind, she had richly deserved. Not only that, she'd been busted down a rank to Sergeant and split up with her boyfriend. Married boyfriend, as Joanna pointed out. "Good riddance."

Things had started to look up when a prominent community member was murdered at the Sea Breeze Marina a few months ago. She'd thrown herself into the investigation with gusto, and for a short while and for the first time since she'd moved to Shell Bay, Linda had felt almost... happy.

But that was in the distant past now, and Linda was getting grouchy. Spending time with Joanna had lifted her spirits, but as her friend had driven away the previous evening, so had her enthusiasm and newfound appreciation of the small town.

As Linda sat on the side of her bed and massaged her forehead, another waft of cigarette smoke made her gag.

"Agnes," she shouted again. "Go away." The dingy, one-bedroomed suite attached to Agnes' house was once inhabited by Agnes' mother who, like

Agnes, was a chain smoker. Linda had abandoned her attempts to get rid of the yellow stains on the walls and paintwork but had at least eliminated the musty odour of stale tobacco by continuously leaving the windows open. But she couldn't stop Agnes from prowling around with her perpetual cigarette squeezed in the corner of her mouth. There was no reply. Linda heard a shuffling sound and then a wheeze followed by a hacking cough.

Linda sighed again. It was time to get up anyway.

In half an hour, Linda was showered, dressed, and holding her first coffee of the day. She stood on the front step of her apartment and savoured a mouthful. It was a beautiful late September morning. The slight chill in the air was the first hint of fall, but the azure blue sky promised another warm day. A gull floated overhead, and the salty tang in the breeze reminded Linda of how close she was to the ocean. Maybe living in Shell Bay wasn't so bad after all, she thought as she breathed in a lungful of the sea air. And then choked.

Agnes materialised beside Linda, engulfed in her usual cloud of cigarette smoke.

"Morning, Agnes," Linda said, but Agnes completely ignored her.

"Good morning," Linda said a little louder and rolled her eyes as she noticed Agnes was wearing wired earbuds attached to her smartphone.

"You'll be off to work then," Agnes said loudly in her raspy voice, sounding as if all she'd done her entire life was drink whisky in smoke-filled lounges. She squinted at her phone and tapped at the screen before removing the earbuds.

Agnes was of indeterminate age. It was impossible to tell how long she had lived because her face had been ravaged by years of chain-smoking. It was lined and crinkled and looked like a scrunched-up yellowing paper bag, apart from Agnes' two beady black eyes. Her lips were thin and almost invisible, so the protruding cigarette was the only indicator of her mouth. Her bony fingers were stained yellow by nicotine, and her voice was low and gravelly. Agnes was thin as a rake—probably, Linda thought, because the woman seemed to exist on coffee and cigarettes—but there was nothing frail about this woman. Her whole attitude was combative. There was a rumour in town that Agnes Crofton killed her own mother, who was, on all accounts, a mean old woman, and Linda could well believe it.

Agnes also seemed to know everything that was going on in Shell Bay and everyone's business. She knew who was getting a divorce, who was having an affair, which of the children were 'born on the wrong side of the blanket', as she put it, and she revelled in human misery.

Agnes peppered Linda with constant questions about the cases she was working on. It didn't matter how often Linda told her that her work was confidential, Agnes ignored her. She was not shy about offering her opinion and unsolicited advice on how Linda should do her job. Agnes Crofton was a complete pain in Linda's butt. On the other hand, Linda conceded, Agnes' local knowledge was second to none. Her nosiness and dedication to ferreting out everyone's private business had actually been an asset to Linda during the murder investigation.

"Yes, I'm off to work," Linda said, taking another gulp of coffee and thankfully feeling her headache recede a little. "What are you listening to?"

"They'll be happy to have you back, I suppose." Agnes sniffed, ignoring Linda's question and taking a long drag of her cigarette without removing it from her mouth.

"What do you mean?" Linda asked suspiciously. Agnes rarely gave her a compliment. Linda watched in fascination as the cigarette burned almost to the end, a long trail of ash suspended in midair.

"They'll be happy to have you back," Agnes repeated with an amused glint in her eyes, "given that someone just fished half a corpse out of the marina."

Chapter Three

Sea Breeze Marina was familiar to Linda. It was where Commodore Hiscocks, a pompous, self-proclaimed 'pillar of the community', had been murdered shortly after Linda had joined the Shell Bay RCMP Detachment.

As Linda drove to the marina, she remembered how delighted she'd been at having a nice, juicy murder to investigate. Hoping that a quick closure of the case would lead to a transfer back to Victoria and the reinstatement of her rank.

Neither of these things had happened, and Linda did have the good grace to feel some shame about being so focused on how the death of a human being could potentially help her career.

The residents of Shell Bay had been shocked about the murder of Commodore Hiscocks. The investigation had not been straightforward. First, Linda's efforts had been hampered (unintentionally) by Constable Ray Reynolds, who had no experience investigating a murder case. Linda often wondered about Ray's policing experience, which seemed to be limited to giving a good 'talking to' to teenage bicycle thieves and, recently, issuing parking tickets outside the cafe, while purchasing the daily Mocha Choca Crunch Muffins for the morning briefing at the detachment.

Still, Linda had to admit that Ray had helped, albeit accidentally, with his local knowledge.

Second, Linda's case had been complicated by the interference of a group of liveaboards at the marina who called themselves 'Wharf Rats'. Sarah Cooper, Jewell Winslow, and Joseph Jackson (who at one point had been the prime suspect) had been determined to meddle, and although Linda had to concede that Sarah Cooper had solved the murder first, the amateur sleuth had nearly been drowned by the killer. Linda had saved her.

Last, the whole case had dredged up secrets from Shell Bay's past and had been personally embarrassing for the mayor and Staff Sergeant Croud. Neither of them had fully recovered, especially as Shell Bay had been top of the list for so-called 'murder tourists' to visit over the summer.

As Linda parked her car in the marina parking lot and then marched down the ramp to the docks, she imagined how anxious Croud would be at the appearance of another corpse.

Linda had expected to push her way through reporters held back by crime scene tape on the docks and to see crime scene technicians bustling about their business. Instead, the marina was deserted save for gulls screeching and a curious harbour seal bobbing in the tide at the bottom of the boat ramp.

"What the..." Linda muttered and wondered if this was Agnes' idea of a prank. Then she saw a tall figure slowly exiting the new restaurant, Dine on the Dock. The familiar figure paused and seemed to be biting into a large sandwich, oblivious to Linda approaching.

"Ray," Linda snapped when she was a few feet from him. "What the hell is going on? Agnes told me... I mean, I got a report that a corpse... I mean, there has been some kind of discovery down here?" She faltered, not wanting to look like a total idiot if Agnes had, in fact, been pulling her leg.

"Oh, hi, Sarge," Constable Ray Reynolds said, just before taking another bite of the large sandwich he was holding.

"Why didn't you call me in?" Linda demanded. "If a body has been discovered, we need all hands on deck," and she shook her head in irritation at her unintended pun as Ray grinned.

"Good one, Sarge."

"Well?"

"It was your day off, Sarge," Ray said, his mouth full and the greasy contents of the sandwich dripping down the front of his shirt. "Didn't want to bother you on a day off. Besides," he said, waving the hand that held the sandwich and narrowly missing splattering Linda with what looked like mustard, "It wasn't a whole body. Just an arm, Sarge. In fact," he winked at Linda, "it was all hands on deck, get it?" He laughed at his own joke. "One hand, anyway."

"What?" Linda said, her voice rising in annoyance. "A human arm?"

"Er, that's what I said, Sarge," Ray said, his tone relaxed. "A human arm in a crab trap. Did you have a lovely weekend, then?"

"Yes, I did," snapped Linda. "I mean, none of your busine... Oh, for God's sake, what are you eating?"

Another blob of yellow goop slid down Ray's chin and deposited itself on his shirt collar.

"Seafood in a bun," he said in a muffled voice as he chewed on his last bite. "Trying it out for Joseph," he said proudly, as if the owner of the newest eatery in Shell Bay had bestowed him with the greatest honour of his life.

Linda sighed.

"You need to tell me everything," she said, feeling her headache, which had receded, make a comeback. She fished in her pockets for her sunglasses and realised that, in her haste to leave, she'd left them at home. "But first, I need a coffee."

Dine on the Dock Seafood Restaurant wasn't open for breakfast. Joseph, the new owner, had come to an agreement with The Bean Express, which, until now, enjoyed the entire patronage of Shell Bay. Joseph wouldn't interfere with their breakfast trade if they didn't open for evening meals. At lunchtime, it was everyone for themselves. As it happened, neither establishment had suffered. In fact, having two places to eat in Shell Bay attracted more visitors and an increase in revenue for everyone.

This morning, the restaurant doors were unlocked, and Linda could smell freshly brewed coffee.

The restaurant used to be the marina office. It had been a ramshackle building, resting on a worn dock in the middle of Sea Breeze Marina. Now, despite its refurbishment, it was still shabby, but Joseph Jackson, the owner, with help from his eccentric friend Jewell, had transformed it.

The tables and chairs didn't match. The walls were festooned with driftwood artwork and fishing nets. The main counter was painted bright yellow, and the menu was chalked onto a blackboard that hung from the ceiling. The result was eclectic but oddly satisfying. Even Linda, who usually preferred modern lines and chrome accents, had to admit the place oozed quirky charm. And the seafood was spectacular.

However, Linda couldn't help glancing at the corner of the restaurant where the marina manager's desk had once stood. An image of the dead body of Commodore Hiscocks, lying in a pool of blood, popped into her mind. She shook her head, as if to dislodge the thought, and made herself focus on today's discovery. Or yesterday's discovery, as she reminded herself in annoyance.

Linda hated being a step behind in an investigation. Still, there was nothing she could do except catch up quickly.

Three people were sitting at one of the restaurant tables, with mugs of coffee in front of them and large sandwiches on a plate that looked a lot like the one Constable Ray Reynolds was still munching on.

Sarah Cooper, Jewell Winslow, and Joseph Jackson were the Wharf Rats. Although the term sounded derogatory, Ray explained to Linda that it just meant people who hung about a lot at docks or marinas. These three had embraced the label.

Sarah Cooper, a fifty-something, pleasant-looking woman with a ready smile, was the newest addition to the wharf rat community. She'd moved from the mainland with an idealistic dream of living on her own boat, watching the sun go down every night with a glass of wine and a good book. Almost as soon as she arrived at Sea Breeze Marina, she'd stumbled across the bloody corpse of Commodore Hiscocks, and her dream had turned into a nightmare. It hadn't deterred Sarah though. To Linda's immense irritation, Sarah fancied herself as an amateur detective, having spent her career as a secretary for Thurgood's Private Investigation Inc. in Vancouver. Her meddling had nearly cost her, her life. but her investigation skills had been helpful, Linda reminded herself.

Linda had also butted heads with Jewell and Joseph at the beginning of the Hiscocks case. Joseph had initially been a suspect due to an incident in his past when he'd worked as a chef at a busy restaurant. In a moment of high stress, he hit a sous chef with a rolling pin after the unfortunate member of staff had spilled hot soup all over Joseph. It had all been a misunderstanding, and once the murder had been solved, Joseph had harboured no hard feelings towards Linda.

Sarah waved at Linda to join them.

"Detective Sergeant," Joseph called out to her. "Come and try my new Seafood in a Bun."

Linda and Ray joined the trio at the table. "Just coffee for me," Linda said, not relishing seafood at breakfast time. Joseph got up and fetched the coffee urn and a mug for Linda, and poured everyone a fresh one.

Jewell didn't acknowledge Linda at all. She seemed to be gazing into the distance, lost in thought. Then Linda noticed the earplugs attached to Jewell's phone, just the same as Agnes this morning.

She was about to ask Jewell what she was listening to when Sarah asked, "So you're here about the arm? I felt so sorry for that poor man who caught it in his crab trap. He was so shocked."

"Which man?" Linda demanded and turned to look at Ray.

"I was going to tell you, Sarge," Ray said in a soothing tone. "Once you had your coffee."

Linda closed her eyes and mentally counted to ten. Or it might have been out loud. Either way, Constable Ray Reynolds had two speeds: slow and stop. When Linda had first arrived at Shell Bay, Ray had been suspicious of the new Sergeant. Word had reached the small detachment that Linda Jenkins was an overly ambitious pain in the rear end who didn't work well with others. It wasn't an inaccurate description, and for the first weeks, Ray and Linda clashed.

But since the Hiscocks murder, when they were forced to work together, Ray and Linda had come to an understanding of sorts. Linda was more patient with the way policing worked in a small community, and Ray... well, Ray hadn't changed at all, really. But Linda found him less irritating. Most days, anyway.

"It's probably someone who fell overboard," Ray said confidently, wiping his mouth with a napkin.

"Wouldn't someone have noticed?" Sarah asked. "How long has the body been down there? I expect there are all kinds of lab tests the police can do these days, aren't there?" She looked questioningly at Linda.

"Can we go back to the beginning, please?" Linda asked. "How did this man come to pull up part of a dead body in the first place?"

"It was yesterday afternoon," Sarah said. "I was settling myself down with a book. It's been such a long time since I had a good read, so I made myself a cup of tea. It was too early for wine, even though I can have wine whenever I want... Oh." Sarah noticed Linda scowling at her and making circular motions with her hand, indicating that Sarah should get to the point of this story quickly.

"Anyway, a young man asked if he could drop a crab trap off the end of the dock. I said yes, and he did. Then he went away and came back a couple of hours later and pulled it up. Voila! An arm in the trap." She shuddered at the memory. "It was all swollen and had ragged edges."

"That'll be where the crabs chewed on it," Joseph said. "They eat anything."

"And then you called the detachment?" Linda asked. "And did the man wait?"

"Oh, yes," Sarah said. "Ray came down right away, and then the forensic people, and then..."

"I took him in for questioning, as per procedure," Ray said, eyeing up the plate of sandwiches. "But the poor fella was in shock. He just wanted a nice fat crab for dinner. I processed him properly, Sarge. No priors or anything. Just an unlucky bugger who wanted a nice feed of crab."

"Right," Linda said, pleased that Ray had followed procedure but making a mental note to check his work. Just in case. "And the arm is at the lab now?"

Ray nodded, his mouth full of his second Seafood in a Bun. "And I also contacted the police divers," he said, "to see if there are any more remains down there," he added when he'd swallowed. "That's all right, isn't it, Sarge?" He looked anxiously at Linda.

"That's great work, Ray," Linda said, and she meant it. Maybe the constable was getting the hang of police work after all. "When will they be here?"

"Any minute, Sarge," Ray said. "Oh, I forgot. Croud wants to see you. Er, as soon as you get in," he added.

Linda rolled her eyes. Staff Sergeant Croud was more an administrator, in Linda's opinion than a real policeman, and he would probably be freaking out about the budget, especially with the cost of police divers.

"Right then," Linda said, gulping down her coffee. "You stay and wait for the divers. Call me when—or if—they find something."

"Righto, Sarge," Ray said.

"They won't find anything," Joseph said. "It was lucky to find the arm. Crabs do all the garbage clean up on the ocean floor. They eat dead marine life, sewage, human bodies... anything."

Linda stood up and fixed Joseph with a firm look. A thought had just struck her. She pointed at the plate of sandwiches, now depleted. "So what 'seafood' is in those buns?" she asked.

A slow flush moved up Joseph's neck. "Well, er, all sorts..." he started to bluster.

"Joseph?" Linda didn't let him off the hook.

"Okay then, I had lots of crab in the freezer, and there's no way I can sell crab cakes now, is there?" he said defiantly.

"Oh, no," Sarah said, and she pushed her half-finished bun away from her, her face turning a pale shade of green.

"Thought so," Linda said and turned to walk away, relieved she had stayed away from the 'seafood' in a bun.

Chapter Four

When Linda arrived at the detachment, Wenda, the receptionist, was leaning back in her chair with one leg resting on the desk. She was studiously painting her toenails and didn't bother to look up.

"You're late. He's waiting for you," she said, dispensing with any small talk, as she jerked her head in the direction of Staff Sergeant Croud's office.

"I've been down at the Marina," Linda said, "getting up to speed on the case."

"Just some hobo fell in the water and drowned," Wenda said confidently, switching her legs and starting on the other set of toes. "Happens all the time."

"Well then," Linda said sarcastically as she headed towards Croud's office, "case closed."

Croud was pacing the room when she entered after knocking first.

"Where have you been?" Croud demanded, stopping to glare at her.

"At the marina, sir," Linda answered. "Constable Reynolds got me up to speed on the case, and he seems to have everything under control, so I thought I'd—"

"Case? What do you mean 'case'?" Croud resumed his pacing. He was a small man with a narrow face and a slightly hooked nose. When he was pacing back and forth, which he did whenever he was anxious, his head bobbed slightly, and he reminded Linda of a crow pecking at the ground.

"Well, sir, we've found human remains. We'll have to identify them and then ascertain if foul play was involved in the person's demise or if it was an accident," Linda said, trying to keep her voice both reassuring and reasonable.

"Foul play?" Croud said, startled. "What do you mean, foul play? It's surely just some hobo—"

"Who fell in the water and drowned?" Linda finished for him. "Possibly, sir. But we won't know until we properly investigate."

"Dear Lord, not another murder," Croud uttered and shot a look upwards at the ceiling, as if summoning divine intervention. "The cost... Did you know that idiot Reynolds has called in a diving team? He's blown my budget. And then there are the lab costs, and if it turns out to be a murder, there'll be all sorts of forensic costs—"

"Sir," Linda said as soothingly as she could, "I'm sure it will turn out to be an accident. But think of this. We'll be able to bring a family's tragedy to an end. To provide closure. We'll have spared no expense to fulfill our duty to the public."

"Hmm." Croud stopped pacing and stroked his chin, imagining the headlines, no doubt, Linda thought.

She hoped it would be a murder. It was callous of her, she knew, but she didn't join the police to direct traffic and help old ladies cross the road. She wanted to put bad guys behind bars, smash international crime rings, and destroy drug cartels. It was a miracle that Shell Bay had already offered up one high-profile case, so now that a body part had turned up unexpectedly, Linda thought she had to make hay while the sun shone.

Besides, it had been months since the last murder, and she was getting bored.

She did feel a bit sorry for Croud, though. He'd quite happily worked his way up the ranks without incident for his entire career and was now looking forward to retirement. The Hiscocks case had caused him some embarrassment, as Croud's nephew had been somewhat involved in the investigation, and there had been a few secrets unearthed, which Croud would have preferred to leave buried. All in all, the top brass had been quite pleased with the result.

Unfortunately, Shell Bay had been spotlighted in the media for all the wrong reasons, and various reporters had written 'in-depth' articles about Croud's involvement with a biker gang in his youth.

Linda knew how Croud felt. Journalists had probed into her past and the unfortunate incident in Victoria, which had led to her demotion and posting to Shell Bay.

"You let me know what the divers find," Croud said after a few moments of anxious silence and head bobbing, "and whether the lab can find any clue to the identity. DNA or whatnot," he said, waving his hand.

"We'll only be able to identify the remains if the DNA is in the system," Linda reminded him. "I'll start by looking through missing person reports once I have an idea of how long the remains have been in the water."

"Right, right, get on with it then," Croud said, sitting down at his desk with a sigh. "But no more ordering up divers and tests or anything else without checking with me first."

Chapter Five

Sarah Cooper watched Detective Sergeant Linda Jenkins leave the restaurant. She gazed at the half-eaten Seafood in a Bun on the plate in front of her and felt slightly queasy.

It wasn't the crab. It was the image of the arm in the crab trap, grey flesh half sliding off the forearm, the fingers blue and swollen with water, and the bone showing where sea life had picked away at it. The only indication that the arm was once attached to a human being was a metal ring, embedded in the knuckle of the ring finger. It was the left arm. Not that it mattered, Sarah supposed. She also thought it was likely that it was a man's arm. It was large, and the ring was a masculine design.

Poor soul.

Sarah hoped the police would find out who the man was, and how and when he died. Then maybe, her mind would allow the image to fade away.

Constable Ray Reynolds was arguing with Joseph, who was insisting that although the Seafood in a Bun contained crab, it had been frozen, and he was merely using it up 'until the fuss blows over'.

"But where did you get the crab?" Ray was demanding. "Whereabouts did it come from?"

"I dunno," snapped Joseph. "I didn't ask for their address when I pulled the traps up."

Jewell was oblivious to everything going on around her. She had small white earplugs in her ears and was holding her phone in her lap.

Sarah sighed.

Jewell had been behaving strangely for a while now. After the Hiscocks' murder and Sarah's near-drowning, the three of them, Jewell, Joseph, and Sarah, had spent much of the summer together. It had been fun, helping Joseph with his restaurant plans and drinking wine in the evenings, watching the sun go down over the marina. But lately, they had all drifted apart. Joseph was busy with Dine on the Dock, of course. But Jewell was preoccupied too. Whenever Sarah had suggested walking into town or morning coffee together, Jewell had been too busy and sometimes didn't even bother answering Sarah's texts or funny good morning gifs.

Jewell had been the first one Sarah had told about the arm—after the police, of course. She hoped the discovery of another body (although as yet, a partial body) at Sea Breeze Marina might prompt a little of the old camaraderie of the Wharf Rats. But Jewell had been dismissive. "Probably a drunk who fell in," she said and waved her hand. "Happens all the time."

She rolled her eyes when Sarah had suggested doing a little investigating of their own.

"Best let the police get on with it," she said, and that was that.

Sarah was surprised to see Jewell in the restaurant that morning. But Jewell hadn't said much; she'd just continuously glanced at her phone as if she were waiting for a call, and now, Sarah assumed, Jewell was listening to a podcast. The only times she'd talked to Sarah recently was to tell her about the true-crime podcast which was going 'viral' (whatever that meant, Sarah wasn't sure) in Shell Bay.

"Have you listened to it yet?" Jewell had demanded. "You should. It's all about what happened here. Every little thing."

"Why on earth would I listen to that?" Sarah had asked, genuinely bewildered. "I was here. I know what went on."

"Yes, but the Shadowcaster has done interviews with loads of people who give their opinions about the Commodore's murder."

Sarah still hadn't got it. "Everyone is entitled to their opinion, I suppose. But I'm not sure I want to listen—"

Jewell had snorted. "You don't know what you're missing."

Sea Breeze Marina was famous. Or maybe 'infamous' was a better word. It had been the scene of a gruesome murder that had set off a chain of events in Shell Bay, culminating in one more murder of Shell Bay's most notorious criminal, and the unveiling of some unsavory scandals in the small town's past. Sarah, newly retired to the community and living on her first-ever boat at Sea Breeze Marina, had been up to her neck in all the drama, as it had been her who had discovered the first body. She practically tripped over the corpse of Commodore Hiscocks in the old marina office. Of course, it had all been refurbished, but it had taken Sarah a while before she could enjoy a meal in the restaurant without visualising poor dead Commodore Hiscocks lying in a pool of blood in the corner.

Sarah's involvement in the whole affair might have been limited to just being the unlucky person who discovered the first body, had Sarah not been prompted to start an unofficial investigation after Joseph Jackson, one of the liveaboards and now restaurant owner, had been wrongfully identified as the prime suspect.

Before Sarah had retired to Sea Breeze Marina, she worked for Thurgood Investigations Inc., although not as one of their investigators. She'd been the secretary and receptionist, a detail she'd glossed over when Jewell and Joseph had asked for her help. Sarah had obliged, and although she identified the killer before the police, she'd nearly been killed. It was only the brave actions of Detective Sergeant Linda Jenkins that saved her.

Sarah had told her story many times to interested visitors seeking out the scenes of crime at the marina and Shell Bay. It had been a busy and noisy summer. Because of the town's newfound notoriety, there had been an uptick in tourists. All of them, it seemed, were armed with cell phones, taking pictures and videos of the marina and other notable landmarks and badgering the residents for morsels of information they couldn't glean from press reports.

At first, it had been fun. Taking selfies, signing newspaper articles, and accepting free coffee and muffins in exchange for answering the same questions from inquisitive strangers over and over again. But Sarah was tired of it now and had been glad that all the 'murder tourists', as Fiona Driver, the new marina manager, called them, were losing interest.

But then a true-crime podcaster got wind of the story. The Shadowcaster, as he called himself, 'dropped' a new episode every week about a crime story that was playing out in the news. He prided himself on ferreting out the 'story behind the story' by interviewing people close to the crime—his anonymous sources. Everyone in Shell Bay was talking about the Shadowcaster. The identity of the sources was hotly debated, and Sarah had been accosted several times when she'd been in town and accused of selling her story. The Shadowcaster had not contacted her at all. Sarah thought this a little strange, given her involvement. Instead, the faceless podcaster seemed satisfied with creating content that was light on facts and heavy on provocative, sensational speculation.

Shell Bay loved it.

And now, there was 'breaking news' in Shell Bay yet again. A poor soul had suffered a watery demise and was no doubt about to become the star of the Shadowcaster's macabre (and slightly vulgar, in Sarah's opinion) entertainment broadcasts.

"More coffee?"

Joseph's voice broke into Sarah's reverie. He was standing over her, holding the nearly empty coffee pot.

"Oh, no thanks."

Sarah looked around. Jewell had disappeared and left Sarah sitting alone. The remains of the seafood sandwiches now limp and soggy on the plate.

Joseph sighed and sat down beside Sarah.

"I suppose I should ditch all the crab in the freezer," he grumbled. "I'll have to change the menu, and I've just spent a fortune getting them printed and laminated."

"This will all blow over soon," Sarah said as she patted his arm. "This will be old news in a couple of days, you'll see."

"Not if that damn podcast thingy gets hold of it," Joseph moaned. "Why do people listen to that thing? Haven't they got better things to do with their time?"

"People love drama," Sarah said simply. She had to admit, she was a big fan of all the murder mystery shows on TV, the true crime and the fictional stuff. And she loved nothing more than spending an afternoon reading a gory crime story. "Jewell seems to enjoy it," she sighed. "I haven't seen much of her at all this summer."

"Oh, it's not just the podcast," Joseph said, standing up and picking up the plate of leftover sandwiches. "I would have thought you'd have noticed, being the famous investigator of Shell Bay."

"Noticed what?"

Joseph grinned at her and winked before turning to go back into the restaurant kitchen and calling over his shoulder, "Jewell Winslow has a boyfriend."

Chapter Six

Mayor Gordon Godson sat upright in his chair behind his desk, one hand clutching a mug of coffee and the other balling up pieces of paper and throwing them absentminded into the waste bin beside his chair. He didn't hear the tap at his office door, or the louder knock, or the impatient rapping that followed, accompanied by a voice calling out, "Mayor Godson? Are you alright?"

Gordon jumped when the door burst open and his assistant strode up to his desk, glaring with her hands on her hips. "Mayor. Didn't you hear me knocking?"

Gordon removed the tiny earplugs from his ears. "What is it, Karen?" he said irritably. "I'm busy. And would you mind knocking before—"

"I did... Never mind." His assistant closed her eyes briefly as if summoning inner strength. "Mayor, have you signed those cheques? They need to go out today."

"What cheques?"

"I left them right there on your desk." Karen pointed.

Gordon looked down at the pile of documents and realised he'd been crumpling the checks into tiny balls and tossing them away. "Oh," he said. "Er..."

His assistant looked at him incredulously when she saw what the mayor had done. Then, with effort, she rearranged her expression into one of concern. "Mayor, are you feeling okay? Do you need a moment to meditate or something?"

Mayor Godson thought he detected a slight note of sarcasm in Karen's voice, but when he looked up, her facial expression remained fixed.

"No, I... I was just listening to that podcast, you know, the true crime one about Shell Bay and Hiscocks and all that..."

"Mayor." Karen's voice was firm as if she were the Mayor's mother dishing out tough love. "You have got to put all that behind you. It was tragic, but the police solved the case and the murderer is behind bars. The whole thing was traumatic for all of us, but it's in the past now. We have to look forward. *you* have to look forward. For all our sakes."

Gordon sank back into his seat. "You're right, of course," he mumbled.

The thing was, it wasn't the murder that played on his mind, as horrible and scary as it had been. It was the whole scandal surrounding it. Once upon a time, Gordon Godson had been the lead singer for the Neon Dreamers, an '80s boy band. They had topped the charts and done a whirlwind tour of Canada. Well, they hadn't quite topped the charts, and they had only played a couple of venues before the tour was cancelled, but still, Gordon had been famous. The most famous son of Shell Bay who had triumphantly returned to his hometown, married his actress wife, Maria, and become mayor. Local boy made good. Except it was all based on a lie. Not his lie. But a lie all the same.

Gordon Godson's pop star career had started when he won the Shell Bay talent contest. It had been the pivotal moment in his life. Except the contest had been rigged. Gordon had been 'chosen' as the winner because of his clean-cut good looks, not his singing talent. In fact, he recently discovered that the judges thought he 'couldn't hold a tune in a bucket'. But the music agent had needed a certain type to lead the Neon Dreamers, so the fix was in. That decision had set off a series of unintended consequences, culminating in the murder of Commodore Hiscocks over twenty years later. Now, Gordon wasn't sure what to do or how to feel. His whole life, his whole identity was in question. Every time he walked down Main Street he sensed people looking at him, judging him.

He'd tried to talk to his wife about how he felt. "Oh, darling," she'd said, "I always knew you couldn't sing. I married you anyway."

Gordon had buried himself in his work. He was still the mayor of this town, so he'd be the best mayor he could be. He rallied the town councillors and they approved grants for Sea Breeze Marina, changed bylaws to allow more liveaboards, and issued a permit for the new restaurant. The summer had been a great success. Sure, many of the tourists had come because of the murder and scandal, but the business owners hadn't cared. They had reported their highest revenues in years. Gordon was starting to feel better, and people had stopped sniggering when they saw him. And then, last week over breakfast, he'd been dragged back into despair.

"Have you heard this new podcast everyone's talking about, darling?" Maria asked casually as she poured Gordon's freshly squeezed orange juice.

"Podcast? Nope," Gordon replied. He never listened to podcasts. He didn't have the attention span. Two minutes in and he was wondering about what to have for lunch, or why there were so many complicated rules he had to follow in council meetings. What was a motion anyway? And why did two people have to pass one?

"It's all about Shell Bay, darling," Maria said. "You should listen. The podcaster mentions you a lot."

And so Gordon had binged the first three episodes.

The podcast—Shadowcaster's Sinister Symposium—was a true crime series. Shadowcaster himself had a deep rumbling voice, not unlike Morgan Freeman. 'Murder at the Marina' was a series of eight episodes dedicated to 'peeling back the complex layers of a real-life crime which terrified a tiny coastal community'. It wouldn't have been so bad if Shadowcaster had merely reported the events as they had occurred, but he had interviewed numerous people in the community, many who had given their unvarnished opinion of their mayor's fraudulent fame. "I remember that talent contest," one woman had declared. "Nobody in their right mind thought Gordon had won. He sounded like someone had trod on a cat's tail."

Gordon became aware that Karen was still standing in front of him. He noticed that her facial expression was somewhere between exasperated and sympathetic.

"Sorry," he muttered. "You're right."

"How many episodes have you listened to?" Karen asked, her tone softening a little.

Gordon blushed. "Three," he admitted miserably.

"Now listen, mayor. These things blow over. You know they do. You have made hundreds, no thousands of mistakes and questionable decisions since you became mayor. Nobody can remember all of them. Something else will come along and grab everyone's attention, and this podcaster will move on too."

Gordon looked at his assistant gratefully. "Thanks, Karen. I didn't think of it like that. Would you mind printing those cheques again?"

"Of course, mayor," Karen said, nodding her approval. "And don't you worry. Before you know it, something big will happen and everyone will forget you can't sing."

"I just hope it happens soon," Gordon agreed.

Just then, a young woman barged into the office. Her face was flushed and she was breathless. Both Karen and Gordon turned to look at her.

"Sorry," she gasped. "Sorry to interrupt, but have you heard?"

"Heard what?" Gordon and Karen asked in unison.

"They found another corpse at the marina."

Karen clapped a hand to her mouth in horror.

"Oh my God," Gordon breathed. He couldn't quite believe it. "It's happened already," he exclaimed. "I can't believe it."

"What do you mean?" Karen asked, puzzled.

But Gordon was on his feet. He punched the air in delight. "A corpse," he exclaimed. "A corpse. That's just what I needed." He beamed at Karen. "You were absolutely right. Something big has happened. Call Staff Sergeant Croud and tell him I want to see him tomorrow. We'll arrange a press conference immediately."

Chapter Seven

Sarah had intended to go back to her boat and tidy up the cabin, and then maybe enjoy the September sunshine. But as she left the restaurant, she could see there was a small white tent erected on the dock beside her moorage slip and two men struggling into diver's suits. Constable Ray Reynolds was pacing back and forth along the dock with his phone clamped to his ear.

She sighed. She wouldn't be able to concentrate on her chick-lit while pieces of corpse were being dredged up just a few feet away, so she decided to walk into town for a change of scene. Perhaps the divers would be finished by the time she got back.

It was mid-morning when Sarah reached The Bean Express cafe. She was hungry and could do with another cup of coffee. "A Mocha Chocha Crunch Muffin and a large coffee please." Sarah smiled at Natalie, the cashier.

"No," Natalie said. "Try again."

"Er... pretty please?" Sarah said.

"No, you can't have that order," Natalie said, rolling her eyes and pointing to a notice pinned to the counter. "Due to overwhelming demand, Mocha Choca Crunch Muffins must be ordered a day in advance."

"Oh, right. Then I'll have a Breakfast Wrap," Sarah said, "With extra bacon."

"It's too late for a Breakfast Wrap," Natalie said, pointing to the clock on the wall. "We finish serving those at 11."

"Oh," Sarah said, "But it's only 11:02."

Natalie was unmoved.

"Okay then," Sarah said, glancing at the sparse menu board, "What else have you got?"

"A Lunchtime Wrap," Natalie said.

"What's in that?"

"Scrambled eggs, spinach, tomatoes, bacon, and avocado," Natalie rattled off, looking bored.

"But isn't that the same as the Breakfast Wrap?" Sarah asked.

"No," said Natalie, "We serve the Breakfast Wrap before eleven. It's two minutes past 11, so now we are serving the Lunchtime Wrap. You want extra bacon?"

Sarah nodded and paid. Natalie could be a bit fierce at times, and it was best not to argue with her.

The Bean Express was famous for its Mocha Chocha Crunch Muffins, a delicious flavor combination of coffee, chocolate, and walnuts. Marie Godson, the mayor's wife and self-proclaimed influencer had promoted the muffins on her Instagram account which had well in excess of three thousand followers these days, but the real boost in sales had come when the media had descended on the town during the Hiscocks' murder case. A local reporter had enthused about the muffins on breakfast TV, and since then, The Bean Express had struggled to keep up with the orders. Natalie had taken it upon herself to ration the daily supply, and although she said it was first come, first served, Sarah suspected it had more to do with Natalie's mood and who she found least irritating of all her customers.

The Lunchtime Wrap with extra bacon was delicious and did taste very similar to the Breakfast Wrap. Sarah hoped that nobody would be silly enough to post it on social media, making either wrap as unobtainable as the muffins.

As Sarah sat in the tiny cafe with its polished wooden floors and bright yellow painted walls, covered with local artwork, she contemplated the changes which had occurred in Shell Bay, the marina, and her own life since the Hiscocks murder case. It wasn't just the lack of muffins.

The publicity had embarrassed the mayor of Shell Bay, Gordon Godson. Not only were nefarious activities exposed around a proposed development of the Shell Bay waterfront and Sea Breeze Marina, but the mayor had also faced a personal crisis. Gordon Godson's claim to fame was that in his youth he'd won a talent contest and been picked to be the lead singer of a boy band, the Neon Dreamers. It was a short-lived career but was the core of Gordon's identity. Until recently, he still had the swagger of a rock star and lived, surrounded by reminders of the one short tour and one and only hit song the Neon Dreamers produced.

The murder investigation changed all that. It was revealed that the talent show was rigged, and Gordon Godson's whole life had been based on a lie, as fake as his tan and bleach-blond hair.

There were rumors that during Gordon's subsequent meltdown, he had ripped down a life-sized portrait of his youthful self and had dumped every physical reminder of the Neon Dreamers into the city landfill.

Gordon Godson had thrown himself into the only purposeful role he had left, as the mayor of Shell Bay.

That part of his transformation had mixed results. On one hand, Shell Bay deserved a mayor committed to the economic development of the community, and already Sea Breeze Marina had the restaurant and money for dock upgrades, and other businesses had received municipal grants. On the other hand, Gordon Godson wasn't the sharpest tool in the box, and the gossip in town was that his staff were getting irritated with having to research his latest 'big idea' which changed as often as the wind direction.

For Sarah, the changes since the murder were mainly good ones. She survived near drowning, she solved the murder before the police and was even given grudging credit by Detective Sergeant Linda Jenkins, who had been most irritated by Sarah's meddling, and Sarah was now the proud owner of a smart new boat. And, she reflected, she was part of a unique community, The Wharf Rats of Sea Breeze Marina. It made her feel warm inside, to think she actually belonged somewhere.

Their little marina community was growing. The new marina manager, a lovely woman called Fiona Driver, was competent and efficient.

Because Joseph was now busy with the restaurant, Fiona had employed two young lads to keep the marina clean and tidy and to keep the maintenance up to date.

Fiona had also installed a brand new CCTV system so everyone felt safe.

Sea Breeze Marina had been full of visitors' boats throughout the summer, and Fiona had also designated some more slips for resident moorers, so the liveaboard community had doubled.

It was unfortunate, Sarah pondered, that one newcomer had arrived just two weeks ago, before all the kerfuffle over the arm in the crab trap. The new boat was a converted tugboat, similar to the Misty Blue, Sarah's old boat, and was owned by a good-looking young man who, so far, had kept to himself.

The liveaboards were all moored on the left-hand side of the marina, the port side, as Joseph continuously corrected Sarah, yet the young man had requested a slip on the opposite side. He wasn't unfriendly though; he nodded and responded when Sarah had greeted him yesterday morning.

She didn't know his name yet because he'd been hurrying along the dock when she'd seen him, and he didn't look as if he had time to chat.

Poor man, she thought, whatever must he think of his new home, a half-crab-eaten arm being fished out of the ocean just as he arrived. She, Joseph, and Jewell would have to pay him a visit and reassure him that Sea Breeze Marina was a very friendly and welcoming place, despite the body parts and recent murder.

The other liveaboard arrived nearly two months ago and was a beautifully restored wooden sailboat. The owner was an older man with salt and pepper hair and a white beard, who introduced himself to everyone as Charles D. Harrington. He had a booming voice and loved to chat.

Charles was an interesting man, Sarah thought, full of stories about sailing the high seas and how he'd successfully navigated treacherous storms. She'd been penned into a corner a few times now and had been regaled with his anecdotes. He was also an author, although he hadn't elaborated on what kind of books he actually wrote, and Sarah had never heard of him.

Maybe he wrote under a pen name, she decided as she sipped her coffee and ate her Lunchtime Wrap. Charles seemed very struck on Jewell, she'd noticed. And Jewell, who was often a bit prickly with strangers, had seemed to warm to Charles right from the start.

Could Charles D. Harrington be Jewell's love interest?

Why on earth hadn't she noticed sooner? Jewell had been quiet and keeping to herself, but she exhibited all the usual lovestruck symptoms. Sarah had caught her gazing into the distance with a strange smile on her face, and she hadn't been joining Sarah and Joseph for wine on the deck on Sunday afternoons when the restaurant was closed. She was too busy, she'd said, but hadn't elaborated on what she was doing and who she was with.

Sarah berated herself. What kind of person doesn't notice when their friend is in love?

"Are you finished?" Natalie called. "We need the table for the afternoon rush."

Sarah checked the time. It was two minutes past noon. She looked around. Apart from herself, there were just two elderly gentlemen who seemed to be dozing off over a pot of tea.

It seemed safer to comply with Natalie. Otherwise, Sarah would never get back on the muffin list, so she drained her coffee, and then, in hope of getting back in favour, she delivered her plate and cup to the counter.

Natalie completely ignored her.

Sarah left The Bean Express and stood outside for a moment, wondering what to do next. She supposed the marina would be swarming with policemen and divers for a while longer, and she wanted a few more hours away from the dock to distract herself from the memory of that grisly discovery. Hopefully, by the time she got back to her boat, everything would be back to normal, and maybe the police could identify the poor person who died in such unfortunate circumstances. Sarah shuddered. At least a family would have some closure. That was a comforting thought.

Sarah rummaged in her purse and discovered that she hadn't brought a book with her. She vaguely remembered Jewell telling her that the Shell Bay Bookstore was closed for renovations. How long ago was that? Maybe the store would be open now. She was just about to turn in that direction when she heard a creaking sound, followed by a shout and then a loud crash.

Chapter Eight.

It was just after noon, and Linda finally realised two things. First, she hadn't eaten anything all morning, except a stale muffin that someone had left beside the coffee maker. As she had suspected, her desk was piled with paperwork, which she'd been buried in all morning. Second, she hadn't heard from Constable Ray Reynolds yet. Surely the divers were finished by now?

She sighed. Maybe they hadn't found anything. Maybe Joseph was right, and the crabs had scavenged away all evidence of a corpse, and maybe she'd been too excited at the prospect of another murder to solve. It was just some poor—

Linda's cell phone vibrated on the desk, interrupting her thoughts.

"Ray? What's going on?" she asked when she answered.

Linda listened to Ray's breathless voice and then said, "I'm on my way," before ending the call and hurrying out of the office.

"A skull," Ray said, unable to contain his excitement. "They were down there for hours, and I thought they wouldn't find a thing, but they found a skull. And guess what?"

It had taken less than five minutes for Linda to get from her office to the marina. She found Ray waiting for her at the end of one of the wharf fingers. A white tent had been erected on the dock, and two divers were unbuckling their oxygen tanks, and removing their face masks.

"What?" Linda said, getting annoyed with Ray who was jumping from one foot to another, making the dock sway.

"No, guess..." Ray said, grinning.

"Ray," Linda snapped.

"Oh all right," Ray grumbled, "They found the skull beside a pylon, and there was a cement block with a chain around it, and a few other human bones right beside it."

Linda stared at Ray. "You know what this means?" she said.

"Er... no?" he said, his face creased in confusion.

"It means," a brisk voice said behind them, "that this is most likely a murder."

Linda turned to see Shirley Grimm, the coroner standing there.

"How did you get here so soon?" Linda said, her turn to be confused.

Shirley Grimm—the Grimm Reaper—as she was known, was famous for her efficiency. She had been the coroner for many years, and her team was highly organised and rarely made a mistake. It was Shirley's job to decide whether a death had been the result of foul play or a tragic accident which, as she often said, was made more complicated due to the limitless boundaries of human stupidity.

Shirley nodded at the divers. "They are part of my team. They called me an hour ago, and as luck would have it, I was just down the road dealing with a body found in a freezer. As I can't do much until that corpse has defrosted, I thought I would make a start here."

"And you already think it's murder?" Linda asked, "Surely the concrete block and chain could have been used for anything. To moor a boat or something?"

"Yes. It's up to you to decide if that's evidence or not. No, it's something else. Let me show you."

"You wait here, Ray," Linda said, "and put up some crime scene tape." She'd caught sight of one of the new marina maintenance staff loitering on the dock, clearly curious to find out what was going on.

Shirley led Linda over to the white tent and pulled back the flap. The divers had been depositing their finds onto a white sheet. One of Shirley's forensic team, a young woman wearing a white suit and mask, was examining an assortment of bones, some with little pieces of mottled flesh still attached, Linda noticed, and her stomach flip-flopped.

"Come in, but don't touch anything," Shirley commanded, quite unnecessarily, Linda thought, as it was the last thing on her mind, but she stepped into the tent and then stood still while Shirley pulled on plastic gloves. The coroner then bent over the human remains and picked up the largest piece. It looked like a chunk of grey rock or possibly driftwood, with wispy seaweed stuck to it, until Shirley held it out for Linda to look more closely.

"This is just half of the skull," Shirley said. "See, there is the eye socket. But this is the most important discovery, here."

Shirley Grimm turned over the partial skull and held it out for Linda to see. The wispy seaweed was hair, Linda realised, with a jolt of revulsion.

"Oh. I see what you mean," Linda said. Obvious, even to her untrained eye, was the perfectly round hole in the skull. "Gunshot wound?" she said, looking up at Shirley.

"Unmistakable," Shirley confirmed. "My theory, so far, is that the murderer shot this poor man in the head and then chained his body to a concrete block and dropped him off the side of the dock."

"Man? You're sure?"

Shirley nodded. "Yes. Oh, you didn't see the arm, did you?"

"No, it was my day off," Linda explained.

"A day off?" Shirley repeated as if it was some weird phenomenon. "I never take a day off. I haven't had a vacation in decades. Death doesn't take a day off, does it, Detective Sergeant?"

"No, I guess not," Linda mumbled, feeling thoroughly chastised, "Sorry."

"Anyway," Shirley continued, "the arm definitely belonged to a man. It also had a ring on one finger. Some kind of signet ring."

"That should help with identification," Linda said. "Anything else? A tattoo maybe?"

Shirley shook her head. "I'll have an approximate age for you when I get these remains back to the lab and do some more testing."

"I don't suppose you have any idea how long ago the body was dumped?" Linda said hopefully.

Shirley smiled. "Nice try, Detective Sergeant. What I can tell you is that it can't be too long. There is still flesh on some of those bones, and crabs don't take long to pick bones clean."

"Less than a month?" Linda pressed.

Shirley rolled her eyes. "Maybe less than a month. But I'm not saying another word until I've done more testing."

"And one of those tests will be DNA?"

"Of course, Detective Sergeant. All invoiced to your budget. Now, if you don't mind we still have work to do." Shirley pointed to the entrance of the tent, indicating that Linda should leave. She didn't need telling twice.

Linda was relieved to be outside the tent. The smell of decay and seaweed, all mixed with something chemical and almost fruity, she thought, was clinging to the inside of her nostrils.

She took a few deep breaths and looked around for Ray. He was nowhere to be seen, and there was no crime scene tape up either.

"Where the heck is he?" Linda said out loud and then saw the constable ambling towards her, his phone glued to his ear.

"Constable," Linda bellowed.

Ray looked up, hurriedly ended his call, and shoved his phone in his pocket.

"Are you alright, Sarge?" he said, "You look a bit green—"

"I told you to put some tape up," Linda said, cutting him off.

"Sorry, Sarge," he said apologetically, "I er... needed to get some crime scene tape... so I was just calling..."

"What's that then?" Linda snapped, pointing at a piece of yellow ribbon poking out from Ray's pocket.

"Oh, er, look at that." Ray blushed and grabbed the ribbon. "It was in my pocket all along. Sorry, Sarge."

"Focus, Ray." Linda was already walking away. "We've got another murder on our hands, and you need to bring your A-game."

Staff Sergeant Croud held his head in his hands as Linda delivered the news.

"Are you sure?" he asked plaintively, "Are you absolutely sure it's murder? Couldn't the hole in the skull have been caused by a rock or something?"

"It wasn't my call, sir," Linda answered, "It was the Grimm Reap... I mean, it was the coroner who deemed it a homicide, sir. It's her decision, as you know."

"Right, right," Croud muttered. "That damn marina... oh," he straightened up, and his face brightened for a moment, "could it be another of that man's victims, you know, James, or whatever his name is? Can we get some kind of confession out of him?"

Linda stared at her staff sergeant. "Sir, the victim could not have been killed by Steven James. The body hasn't been in the water for that long, and besides, are you suggesting that we just get James to confess, so we can clean up the crime stats?"

"Of course not, Detective Sergeant. That's not what I was suggesting at all, I was merely voicing a theory. But it's clear that the marina has attracted some lowlifes and is turning into a hotbed of crime. I'll be bringing that to the mayor's attention, first chance I get." Croud's shoulders sagged again.

"Good idea, sir," Linda agreed. "Now, I'll be needing the conference room. I'll be setting up my murder board in there."

Before Croud could object, Linda turned and left the office.

"Keep me in the loop," Croud called after her.

Chapter Nine

The crash made Sarah jump.

"Sorry," a voice called out, and Sarah looked around to find out where the noise and the apology had come from. It wasn't until she looked up that she saw a man on the top rung of a ladder, wobbling precariously. The ladder was balanced against the front of the Shell Bay Bookstore.

The man seemed to be adjusting the sign above the door, and the twisted metal fragment on the floor below the ladder was the E from Bookstore.

"No harm done," Sarah called to the man, who was slowly making his way down the ladder, feeling for each rung with his feet. When he reached the ground, Sarah could see his face was deathly white and his hands were shaking.

"I'm so sorry," he repeated. "I should have hired someone to change the sign. I'm really not good with heights."

"That's alrig... Oh, I know you," Sarah said in surprise. "You live at Sea Breeze, don't you?"

The man standing in front of her, whose cheeks were gradually returning to a normal pink, was the new liveaboard who had moored on the opposite side of the marina.

He nodded and managed a smile. "That's right. I just moved there. You have The Commodore, don't you?"

"That's right. I'm Sarah Cooper." Sarah stuck out a hand which the man took and shook, although it was quite a feeble handshake, Sarah thought.

"I'm Alex Harding," he said, and then there was an awkward silence. From the fleeting glimpses Sarah had got of Alex Harding at the marina, she'd thought he was very young. He was taller than her and well-built, as if he spent time exercising. But up close, Sarah could see streaks of grey in his dark hair and the beginnings of lines around his eyes. His skin was very pale, even after he recovered from being up the wobbly ladder, and she thought that was odd, given he lived on a boat. Most other liveaboards, even a newbie like herself, had a healthy tan from being outside in all weathers.

"Are you working at the bookstore?" Sarah asked in an effort to continue the conversation. "No, er... I mean yes... I mean, I'm the new owner," Alex said. He gestured at the sign above the door. "I was taking down the old sign because a new one is coming later today. I've been getting ready for a grand opening next week."

"Oh, that's lovely," Sarah said, pleased that for once, she knew something before Jewell, "I love bookstores, and I often browse around this one."

"I hope you'll continue to do that," Alex said, and he smiled. "Why don't you come in and look around? I'm not officially open yet, but I'd like an opinion on some of the changes I've made."

He seemed to have regained his composure.

"If you have time," Sarah said, returning the smile, "I'd love to. I must admit, I wasn't looking forward to going back to the marina just yet, not with all the police there." Then a thought struck her. "Oh, maybe you don't know. About the, erm... discovery."

Alex looked confused. "Discovery? No, I've been getting back to the boat quite late and leaving early because of all this." He waved his hand at the bookstore. "It's taken up all my time, I'm afraid. I haven't had a chance to even introduce myself to all the other liveaboards yet. So, what discovery?"

Sarah sighed. "Not a pleasant one, I'm afraid." She explained about the arm and what had transpired after the crab fisherman had hauled it up in his trap.

"Oh, that's terrible," Alex said, staring at her in horror. Sarah noticed that the color had once again drained from his thin face. "Do they know who it is? I mean, who the arm belonged to?"

"That's what the divers are for, I think," Sarah said, and then, looking closely at Alex she said, "Are you all right?"

Alex swayed a little, and for a moment, Sarah was worried he was about to faint.

He reached out and clutched the ladder to steady himself. The ladder wobbled dangerously, and Sarah grabbed it before it clattered to the ground.

"I think you need to sit down," she said firmly to Alex, who was rubbing his face.

"I'm so sorry," he muttered. "I'm fine. Just climbing up the ladder and then... I'm a bit squeamish," he admitted. "Let me help you with that."

They both maneuvered the ladder so it lay on the ground out of the way.

"Why don't you show me your bookstore?" Sarah said, still concerned about the bookstore owner, whose breath seemed to be erratic and shallow. Alex nodded his agreement.

"I think I need a cup of tea," he said and led her inside.

The bookstore had always been a bit of a jumble. The previous owner, a very pleasant lady, was very helpful and would try to find anything Sarah asked for, but the layout of the shelves hadn't been logical, with non-fiction spilling into the romance section and mystery and thrillers jammed into the travel section. Some of the books had been in alphabetical order using the author's name, and some by the title.

Sarah never minded the dusty chaos. There was nothing better, in her mind than poking around the darkened recesses of quaint, old-fashioned bookstores, breathing in the leathery, musty odor of books that had been unopened for years, and being transported into other worlds by the imaginations and words of writers, which lived on long after they had passed into the next life.

Sarah hoped that Alex Harding's improvements wouldn't include large, gaudy displays of non-book-related novelty objects, like mugs and calendars, which all the modern bookstore chains were now offering, with just a few copies of the latest bestsellers and celebrity cookbooks.

To her relief, all the old charm of the place remained, although everything looked a lot more organised. "Whispering Tide Bookstore," Sarah read on a colourful leaflet displayed on the cashier's counter. "Ooh, is that the new name of the store?"

Alex smiled, and his face lit up. Sarah thought he looked much younger and quite handsome. "Yes. Do you like it?"

"I do. It sounds intriguing and mysterious," Sarah said. "Inviting readers to come in and discover the whispered secrets inside the books."

"That's exactly what I was aiming for," Alex exclaimed. He looked steadier on his feet now. "Come through to the back. Let me make you a cup of tea."

It hadn't been long since Sarah's coffee and wrap, but she was curious to see the rest of the store and wasn't in a hurry to get back to the marina, so she followed Alex past the rows of shelves, mostly full of books that were neatly labeled, she was pleased to see, through a door at the back.

She had to squeeze past a table that nearly filled the tiny room behind the door, which wasn't much bigger than a closet. On the table were boxes of books. At the back of the small room was another open door, and inside, Sarah glimpsed computer equipment scattered on a large table.

"Let me make some space," Alex said as he moved the boxes to one side. "Still getting organised," he explained. In the corner of the room was a kitchen counter and a small sink, and above it, fixed to the wall, were a couple of mismatched cupboards.

Alex reached up and took out a kettle and filled it. In a few minutes, the kettle was making gurgling sounds, and Alex had dropped teabags into two mugs.

"So, tell me more about this... er, body part? The arm?" he asked when he handed Sarah a mug. "Sorry, hope you don't mind black tea. I don't have any milk," he apologised.

"Oh, that's fine," Sarah smiled. She gestured to the open door. "It looks like you are going all high tech," she said. "The last lady used to scribble book orders on the back of envelopes. Sometimes she'd forget the order, and I had to come in several times to remind her. I don't think she even had a phone."

Alex looked confused for a moment. "High tech?"

"Your computers," Sarah explained and nodded towards the open door.

"Oh, right." Alex moved swiftly to close the door.

"Let's sit in the bookstore," he said. "There's more room out there."

Sarah followed Alex into the back of the store. In the corner were two leather armchairs. "I thought it would be nice to have a reading area for the customers," he explained.

"Lovely idea," Sarah said, sinking into the comfy seat. "But you might not get rid of me," she joked. She drank some of the tea and then set her mug down on a bookshelf beside her.

"Now, do you really want to know about the arm?" she asked. "You seemed quite upset about it."

"I think I should know if there are body parts being pulled out of the ocean where I live, don't you?" Alex said in a joking tone, but his face was serious.

Sarah wondered if he knew about the murder of Commodore Hiscocks and decided that she wasn't going to say anything. Alex Harding looked fine now, but he was clearly quite sensitive, judging by his earlier reaction.

Sarah told him about the macabre discovery the day before and the police response earlier that morning. When she was finished, Alex asked, "So you saw the arm with your own eyes?"

Sarah nodded. "Oh yes, the fisherman pulled the trap up right beside my boat."

"I am so sorry. That must have been awful for you."

Sarah's mind flashed back to Commodore Hiscocks' corpse in the marina office and the crimson pool of blood. Compared to that, the pale, fleshy, sausage-shaped object in the crab trap, even with its ragged edges and swollen fingers, seemed innocuous.

"It wasn't that bad," she said.

"Do you think it was a man's arm?" Alex asked.

It was an obvious question, Sarah supposed. "It was quite large," she said slowly. "If I had to guess, I would say it was a man's arm, yes."

"Were there any distinguishing features?" Alex asked in an almost urgent tone, Sarah thought. "I mean, something that might identify the man. Or person," he quickly added.

"Er, no, not that I saw," Sarah said. "The skin was quite blotchy, from the saltwater" Sarah decided not to tell Alex Harding about the ring on the finger. She didn't know why, but it felt wrong somehow, as if she were telling a secret.

And she was feeling uncomfortable. Alex Harding was gazing at her with an intense frown on his face. It was strange, she thought, all these questions about the arm when only minutes ago, he almost fainted at the thought of it.

"You know, I think I should be getting back," she said. "I'm sure the divers will have finished by now, and hopefully the police will be able to identify the poor soul. Thank you for the tea, and your new bookstore looks wonderful."

The man's expression changed quickly, and he smiled, although it felt insincere to Sarah.

"Of course," he said. "Thanks so much for helping me earlier."

Sarah left the bookstore and stood outside, not sure what to think of Alex Harding. He just spends more time with books than humans, she decided and is a little awkward with new people.

Chapter Ten.

The white tent was still set up at the end of the dock when Sarah returned to the marina. She could see a figure dressed in white overalls talking to Constable Ray Reynolds, and yellow tape prevented her from walking down the dock to her boat. It was all very inconvenient.

The Dine on the Dock restaurant was closed. The marina office, a brand new float house beside the restaurant, was locked, and a notice stuck to the door informed everyone that the marina would be open for business the following day.

Despite the warm September afternoon, there was no activity on the docks, no boaters washing down decks or sharing a beer in the sun. It was all very gloomy, Sarah thought. But then, given that a dead body was being fished out of the ocean, it wasn't surprising.

Sarah decided to check in on Jewell. Maybe she would tell Sarah all about her new relationship. They could gossip over a cup of tea.

The Little Gem, Jewell's boat, was moored three slips down from The Commodore. The cabin door was still shut, and there was no sign of Jewell.

Sarah stepped onto the deck of The Little Gem and rapped gently on the cabin door.

"Jewell?" she called out. "It's Sarah. Are you there?"

Silence. "Jewell?" Sarah tried again. This time, she heard muffled footsteps, and then the cabin door creaked open.

"Jewell, whatever is the matter?" Sarah blurted when she saw Jewell's face. Instead of its usual smooth tan, her face was pale and blotchy, and her eyes were red. Sarah knew immediately that Jewell had been crying.

"I'm fine," Jewell said defiantly.

"No, you're not," Sarah said gently. "I don't need to be a qualified private investigator to see that."

It was a lame attempt at humor, but Jewell sniffed and half-smiled before dissolving into tears. She turned around and went back into the cabin, and Sarah followed her.

"Let me make you a cup of tea," Sarah said. "Get yourself a tissue and sit down, and we'll get you sorted in no time."

Usually, Jewell disliked being organised by anyone else, but to Sarah's surprise, she grabbed a tissue, dabbed at her eyes, and blew her nose noisily while Sarah filled a kettle and popped it on the gas stove to boil.

Jewell sat in one of the armchairs she'd managed to squeeze into the small galley. Her shoulders slumped, and she looked the picture of misery.

"Now, what's this all about?" Sarah asked, opening cupboard doors to find mugs and teabags. "Is it the arm that's got you all upset? Or is it something else?"

Jewell nodded. "Yes," she managed in a croaky voice, and more tears spilled down her face.

Her answer didn't clarify anything, but Sarah waited until the two steaming cups of tea were ready. She put one on a stool beside Jewell and the other on the galley table, and then she arranged some cookies on a plate, taking them from the porcelain cookie jar shaped like a chicken, which looked out of place in the assortment of Jewell's maritime-themed decor.

Sarah sat at the galley table, facing Jewell, and then tried her question again.

"So, which is it?" Sarah asked gently. "The arm, or something else?"

Jewell took a deep breath, making a concerted effort to control her tears before answering. "You know that I've... I've become friendly with Charles Harrington?"

"Yes," Sarah smiled. "Joseph and I are very happy for you."

"Thank you. I have been happy. Until now, that is." A tear formed in the corner of Jewell's eye and rolled down her cheek unchecked.

"What happened?" Sarah asked. "Did you have a fight?"

Jewell shook her head. "Not really. It was all going so well. Charles was such a gentleman. And so interesting... I could listen to his stories for hours..." Her face took on a dreamy look. "He'd travelled all over the world, researching material for his books. He loved to study the history and customs of other civilisations." Jewell's face became more animated. "Did you know that the Yanomami tribe, who live in the Amazon regions of Brazil and Venezuela, have a custom called endocannibalism, which involves consuming the ashes of deceased relatives?"

"Er, no, I didn't know that."

"Well," Jewell continued as if reciting from a textbook, "when a Yanomami dies, the body is wrapped in leaves and placed on a platform where it is left to decompose. After the flesh has decayed, the bones are collected, burned, and ground into a fine ash. This ash is then mixed into a banana soup which is consumed by the entire community during a funeral feast. The Yanomami believe that by consuming the ashes, the spirit and strength of the deceased person are kept within the community and that it helps to assuage their grief. The practice is seen as a way of showing respect for the dead and maintaining a strong connection with their ancestors. Isn't that fascinating?"

"Yes, fascinating," Sarah replied, "but what about Charles? What happened?"

"Oh, yes." Jewell's face dropped again. "We were getting on so well. I really thought our friendship was about to get... more romantic, I suppose." Her face flushed. "It's been a long time since... well, anyway, we were having a glass of wine together about two weeks ago, and Charles was telling me one of his stories, and then he got a call. Usually, he would ignore it, but this time, he looked at the screen and said he had to take it. He went on to the deck, and after a minute, his voice got very loud, as if he was arguing with someone."

"What was he saying?"

Jewell shrugged. "Nothing that made sense. He just said, 'I'm getting nearer to the truth', and then he hung up."

"Gosh," Sarah said. "Who was he talking to?"

"I don't know," Jewell said. "He came back, but he was really distracted. Then the phone rang again, and this time he turned it off, but then he said he was really tired. So I left."

"So who do you think he was talking to?"

Jewell looked sad. "I thought it might be... his wife. I thought he might be married and not have told me. I was really angry, and I didn't sleep that night. Then, in the morning, I was calmer and thought that I was probably overreacting. It could have been anyone, right? And it wasn't any of my business. So, I went to ask him if he wanted coffee, but he wouldn't even open the cabin door. He just shouted out that he was really busy."

"People do get busy, Jewell," Sarah said as reassuringly as she could. "The call might have been about his research, or new book, or something. Maybe he was behind on a deadline. Writers are like that, aren't they? Maybe the call was from his editor or something."

"That's what I told myself," Jewell said. "I went into town and did my grocery shopping, and I even treated myself to one of those new Lunchtime Wraps at The Bean Express. And I felt much better. 'Just give him space, Jewell', I said to myself. 'He's a writer, and those creative types get very emotional. He'll be fine when he's caught up with his work'. But then, I got back to my boat, and found this."

Jewell reached behind her chair and took a piece of folded paper off a shelf. She handed it to Sarah. On one side, in big loopy handwriting, it said "To Jewell."

Sarah unfolded it and read, "To my charming friend, Jewell. It is with great regret that I must end our friendship. It is for the best, I assure you. There are things you don't know about me. Things I cannot tell you for fear it will place you in great danger. Maybe one day, dear Jewell, I will be able to reveal my dark secrets, and you will find it in your heart to forgive me. Until that day, I must bid you adieu. Sincerely, Charles D. Harrington. Goodness." Sarah looked up at Jewell. "What did you do next?"

"I went straight over to his boat, of course," Jewell said, a touch of her old feistiness back in her voice. "I didn't care about danger. But he wasn't on his boat. And he didn't come back, at least, I don't think he did."

"What does that mean?"

Jewell pursed her lips. "I waited on the deck for Charles to come back. I was going to beg him to tell me about the danger and convince him that whatever it was, we would face it together. I waited for hours. It got dark and cold, and it was really late. I went in to get a blanket, and when I came out, I could just make out two figures right by your boat."

Sarah stared at Jewell and felt a tingling sensation go up her spine and lift the hairs on the back of her neck.

"Near my boat? Who was it? Charles?"

"That's what I thought at first. I heard muffled voices, and I thought one of them was Charles. I thought I heard one of them say, 'No, wait', and I was going to call out, but then the figures disappeared beside your boat, and I was distracted by a light going on in Charles' cabin, so I thought those two people might be friends of yours..."

"Friends of mine? That late at night? Nobody came to my boat," Sarah said, feeling a knot of anxiety form in her stomach. "What happened to those people? Did you see them again?"

Jewell shook her head. "No, I got off my boat and went over to have it out with Charles. I was really annoyed by then because he must have passed by my boat and seen the light in my cabin, and he didn't even stop to talk to me."

"So what did he say when you got there?"

Jewell was indignant now. "I didn't talk to him. When I got near, I saw a woman going into his cabin, and then I heard voices."

"So did you confront him?"

"Nooo." Jewell started crying again. "I didn't want to find out he was married. I just crept away and hoped he would come over the next day. But he didn't. And he hasn't been on his boat, and now they found that arm and all the bits of body and I'm really wo-wo-worried."

"Oh, Jewell, I'm sure there's an explanation for all of this." Sarah reached over and squeezed Jewell's hand.

"I know there's an explanation," Jewell said, wiping her eyes. "Either Charles has a wife and he's gone back to her, or he's in bits at the bottom of the ocean and has been eaten by crabs."

She looked at Sarah through the tears rolling down her cheeks. "I really thought he was my... my person. We had so much fun together and I thought he was as happy as me. And he helped me a lot. He fixed my bilge pump."

Jewell swiveled around in her seat, reached behind her, and picked up a photograph frame. She handed it to Sarah.

"See? He looks so happy there, so carefree. This was just after he finished working in the engine room."

Sarah looked at the picture of Jewell and Charles Harrington. They were both laughing at the camera, and Charles had his hand on Jewell's shoulder.

Sarah didn't know if Charles Harrington was happy and carefree or not. It was something else that made her heart sink.

Chapter Eleven.

L inda stuck a note on the conference room door.

'Incident Room' it read, "No Unauthorised Personnel"

She went back into the room and closed the door. She walked over to the whiteboard, picked up a marker, and wrote in big letters at the top, *Murder Board.*

Then underneath, she divided the board into three columns, headed *Victim, Evidence,* and *Suspects.*

Under the victim column, she stuck the photograph of the arm, which Constable Reynolds had taken the day before. He really was getting better at investigating, Linda thought and made a mental note to tell him.

Linda stood back to survey her work. Behind her, the door squeaked. Exasperated, she turned around. "Didn't you see the—"

Staff Sergeant Croud stepped into the room. "What are you doing, Detective Sergeant?" he demanded. "I thought I told you to keep me in the loop. Where's Grimm's written report? You know we can't start an investigation until the coroner has officially declared it a homicide."

Linda stared at him. "But sir, Grimm's report is just a formality. She told me to start investigating—"

"*No!*" Croud practically bellowed at Linda, making her jump. For a moment, they both stared at each other in silence.

"Procedure, Jenkins," Croud said at last, his voice calmer. "Proper police procedure is all I ask for. That's an order."

"Right, sir," Linda said, still a little shaken by Croud's outburst.

Just then, they heard a voice calling out from the reception. "Anyone here? Croud? Anyone?"

"It's the damn mayor," Croud muttered. "I'll have to deal with him," he declared and he left Linda standing in the conference room, staring after him.

In a few moments, she could hear the muffled voice of Mayor Godson. "Croud, I hear we have a murder on our hands. I came right away. We need to call a press conference..." Then Croud's voice.

"Mayor, we need to wait. We haven't had written confirmation it was a murder. In my opinion, it's probably some poor soul who just fell off—"

Then the Mayor again, "Croud, I've been hearing—"

The door to Croud's office banged and Linda couldn't hear any more.

What the hell was wrong with Croud? she wondered. He seemed more uptight than usual. Was he really that anxious about the budget?

"Hmm. Well, if he wants me to follow procedure," she said aloud and picked up her phone. She tapped the screen and started scrolling through her contacts until she found Shirley Grimm's number. She pressed the green icon and then put the phone on loudspeaker.

Linda waited while the phone rang four times before there was a click and the disembodied voice of the coroner echoed through the room.

"You've reached The Grim Reaper. Yes, I know what you all call me. Funny. I am either out of the office or disemboweling a client. Please leave a message and I'll get back to you when I can."

Linda waited until she heard a bleep and then said, "Shirley, it's Linda Jenkins. My boss has a hair up his backside about getting the report before I start my investigation. Do you think you can send something through ASAP? Just what we talked about this afternoon would be great. Thanks very much."

Linda tapped the red icon to disconnect the call.

"There," she said to herself. Then she checked the time. It was late. Wenda and Ray had left over an hour ago. She sighed. There was nothing she could do until the report came through. Shirley Grimm was known as a workaholic, so Linda was sure the emailed report would be waiting for her the next morning.

Linda waved at Barrie, the duty constable who manned the reception when Wenda wasn't there, and then she stepped into the parking lot.

It was nearly seven, and although the sun was still up, the heat was gone and Linda shivered. She considered going back to the marina to chat to Sarah and the other Wharf Rats but quickly rejected the idea. It could wait until tomorrow. It had been a long day.

Linda drove home, and as she pulled into the driveway, she saw the familiar figure of Agnes waiting for her by her front door.

"Of course," she muttered but allowed herself a smile. The old bat was probably dying to know more about the body parts.

Linda parked her car and got out. She waved at Agnes.

"That was very funny," Linda said as she approached Agnes, who had her usual cigarette hanging from one side of her mouth.

"What was funny?" Agnes asked, narrowing her eyes and puffing out a cloud of smoke from the other corner of her mouth which was not occupied by the cigarette.

"The whole 'they've found a corpse' thing, this morning," Linda replied.

"Oh right, that." Agnes continued to puff away.

Linda waited. In the end, when Agnes said nothing further, Linda sighed. She was really tired, she realised. "Are you going to ask me or not? Because if not, Agnes, I really need to go to bed."

"Ask you what?" Agnes said, but wouldn't meet Linda's eyes.

"Ask me about the corpse..." It occurred to Linda that something might be wrong. It wasn't like Agnes to behave like this. Well, it was totally like Agnes to hover around Linda's front door, hoping for a morsel of information, but usually, Agnes wasn't so... furtive about it.

"Is something wrong?" Linda asked.

"No. Why do you ask?" Agnes snapped.

"Because... Oh, never mind." Linda decided that if something was wrong, it was up to Agnes to say. She moved to her front door, put her key in the lock and turned it. Before she pushed the door open, she turned once more to Agnes.

"Are you sure you're okay?"

Agnes gave her a curt nod. Then Linda noticed something. "Agnes, those headphones you're wearing, what are you listening to?"

Agnes seemed to stiffen. "Just a podcast," she mumbled. "No law against it, is there?"

"What podcast?" Linda was intrigued now.

"True crime," Agnes said, and her tone was defensive.

"Oh, right." Linda rolled her eyes. True crime podcasts, in her opinion, were sensational twaddle. People's misery dressed up as entertainment.

"Okay then, Agnes. Good night." Linda pushed her front door open and went into her apartment. She was too tired even to eat dinner, so she went straight to her bedroom, pulled off her clothes, and fell into bed.

"What a weird day," she muttered to herself just before she fell into a deep sleep.

Chapter Twelve.

"Oh, Jewell, I'm so sorry." Sarah hugged the sobbing woman. "It could be someone else with the same ring," she suggested lamely. Jewell shook her head. "What are the chances of that?" She gulped and sniffed. "Two people with the same ring at Sea Breeze Marina? No, it has to be him. It has to be." She cried harder.

Sarah nodded. When Jewell had handed her the photograph, Sarah had recognised the ring on Charles' hand instantly. It was the same as the ring on the arm in the crab trap.

"I don't understand," Jewell sobbed. "What happened to him? How did he end up in the ocean?"

"It must have been an accident," Sarah said, desperately struggling to find some words of comfort for her distraught friend.

"But how? Charles has been around boats and marinas his whole life. He sailed around the world. How could he possibly fall off a dock and drown?"

"He could have been upset," Sarah began, "or stressed, because he loved you, but was married—" But another thought had occurred to her. "Jewell," she said, a hint of nervousness in her voice. "What about the note he sent you? The one when he said he was in danger?"

Jewell stopped crying and wiped her eyes.

"What about it?" she asked.

"Well, if Charles thought he was in danger, and then he had this accident..." Sarah said slowly.

Jewell stared at her. "You mean, he really was in danger? It wasn't just some made-up thing to end our relationship? But what about the woman I heard on his boat?"

"Hmm. Right," Sarah said, but something was bothering her. "When you heard that woman, on Charles' boat, did you actually see her? Or Charles?"

Jewell thought for a minute. "No, but she was talking to him, I heard voices..."

"But do you know for sure she was talking to Charles?" Sarah persisted.

Jewell shook her head slowly. "No, but who else could it be?"

"Jewell, do you remember anything more about the two figures you saw by my boat? Could one of them have been Charles?"

Jewell shrugged. "I don't know. I didn't take much notice, because I thought Charles was on his boat."

Her eyes widened. "You think one of them was Charles? Oh no." She buried her face in her hands. "What if he died right then and I didn't do anything because I thought he was a liar and a cheat?"

"None of this is your fault, Jewell," Sarah said firmly. "Whatever happened to Charles, you are not to blame."

The two women sat in silence, which was only broken by the occasional loud sniff and hiccup from Jewell.

Then Sarah asked, "Do you have any idea why Charles thought he was in danger? If it's true, I mean."

Jewell thought for a minute. "He was very secretive about his work. He was writing about some kind of local history, he said. He always put it away when I was on his boat. He never told me what it was all about."

Sarah rubbed the back of her neck, trying to get rid of a tingling sensation that was getting stronger by the minute.

"What if," she said slowly, "what if Charles was in danger because of his work? What if the woman on the boat was looking for his work? Or his laptop?"

"He didn't have a laptop," Jewell said. "And he never connected to the internet. He was always worried about hackers. He didn't even like me posting his picture on Instagram. That's why I got this picture printed." She gestured to the photograph in the frame. "He didn't text, he always phoned."

"So how did he write?" Sarah asked. "With pen and paper?"

Jewell nodded. "He didn't even type. The only time he talked about his work, he called it his manuscript. He said the only person who would see his manuscript, when it was finished, was his publisher."

Sarah grabbed Jewell's hands in hers. "Jewell, don't you see? Charles didn't have a wife he was hiding from you. He was working on something that put him in danger. Maybe the woman you heard was looking for his manuscript. And maybe those people you saw on the dock that night, maybe..."

"Maybe they killed Charles?" Jewell's face was white now, the blotchiness from her crying having faded, and Sarah thought her friend looked like a ghost.

Jewell held Sarah's hands tighter. "You mean," she whispered, "that Charles was murdered."

Chapter Thirteen.

The next morning, as soon as Linda's alarm went off, she got up. She was relieved that she did not have a headache. An alcohol-free night had resulted in an undisturbed sleep, and Linda felt refreshed. She got out of bed, showered, dressed, and was ready for work in fifteen minutes. She was always energised when she was working on an interesting investigation. She wanted to get into the office early and read Shirley's report, which she was sure would be waiting for her.

Linda sniffed cautiously when she emerged from her apartment, but there was no cigarette smoke. Agnes had definitely been behaving strangely last night. Maybe she had family problems? Did she have family? Linda vaguely remembered Agnes saying something about a sister being a stuck-up bitch. Maybe not family problems then. It just felt like Agnes wanted to talk to Linda about something but didn't know how.

Linda didn't have time right now, but she'd ask Agnes this evening. Agnes was nosy, rude, and sometimes completely objectionable, but Linda couldn't help liking the old bat. Just a bit.

Linda dropped by The Bean Express and, for once, was early enough for Mocha Choca Crunch Muffins, and she persuaded Natalie to sell her four, even though she hadn't ordered them the day before.

"So, is it a murder?" Natalie asked, holding the bag of muffins just out of Linda's reach.

Linda resisted the urge to roll her eyes. Instead, she leaned forward and beckoned for Natalie to get nearer. "Mind your own damn business," she said in a loud stage whisper, and then she snatched the bag out of Natalie's hand before grinning and waving a hand over her shoulder as she left.

"Good luck getting any more muffins," she'd heard Natalie call out.

The muffins were well received when she'd arrived at the detachment. Amazingly, Wenda was already at reception and even managed a smile. Linda frowned when she noticed that someone—probably Croud—had removed the Incident Room notice from the conference door, but at least Constable Ray Reynolds was waiting for her in the conference room.

"Thanks, Sarge," Ray said as he picked up a muffin. "Should I take one to himself?" Ray jerked his head in the direction of Croud's office.

"Wait a sec. Let me check Shirley's email, and then I can deliver her decision at the same time," Linda smiled. At least the muffin would take the sting out of the news for Croud, who was no doubt still fretting about his budget.

Linda quickly left the conference room and went to her desk. She sat down in front of the screen and tapped out her password on the keyboard. When the computer had whirred to life, she could see the little envelope icon at the bottom of the screen, indicating she had an unopened email.

"Excellent," she muttered to herself. "Now I can get on with this investigation."

A minute later, she was staring at the screen, speechless.

"Sarge? Have you got the Grim Reaper's report?" Ray came into the office and stood at Linda's shoulder. "Is that it?"

"Yes and no," Linda said slowly. "I don't know what's going on with Shirley. You were there, weren't you, when she showed me the skull? With the gunshot wound?"

"Nope," Ray said slowly. "I was outside. I didn't actually see it. You told me about it, though," he said hurriedly. "I wasn't eavesdropping or anything."

"Yes, I did tell you," Linda confirmed. "I didn't dream it."

"No, you didn't. You were really squeamish," Ray continued. "I thought you were going to throw up, Sarge. You had this look—"

"Yes, thank you, Ray. The thing is," Linda said, gesturing at the screen, "Shirley said she was going back to the lab to write up a report, and she would confirm the gunshot wound to the skull and officially declare this a murder."

"Didn't she do that?"

"No. This report, which wasn't even done by Shirley, is preliminary and doesn't mention the skull at all."

Linda pulled her cell phone out of her pocket. She scrolled through her contacts until she found the Grim Reaper's one and pressed call. She tapped the loudspeaker button and held her phone, waiting for it to connect. It clicked, and Linda was about to speak when she realised the call had gone to Shirley's voicemail. Except, it wasn't Shirley's bored tone, it was a robotic voice instructing the caller to leave a message. Linda waited for the beep and then spoke.

"Shirley, please call me back. I'm confused about this report. There's no mention of the skull. Is there another report on its way? I need it ASAP. Croud is getting antsy about his budget and is holding up my investigation. Cheers."

Linda ended the call. Then she read the email again and printed off the attachment. She grabbed it out of the printer and scanned it again, hoping she missed seeing a second page. No such luck.

"So, what now, Sarge? Do we wait for the full report? Do we even know if the body is male or female, Sarge?" Ray Reynolds asked, his voice muffled because his mouth was full of muffin. His second muffin, Linda noticed. Now she couldn't even sweeten up Croud.

Linda looked down at the brief report she'd just printed.

"That's just about the only thing we know," Linda sighed. "The body is definitely male. She could tell that from the bones and the ring on the finger."

"Right-o, Sarge, well, that's something. How long had he been down there?"

"This doesn't say. I'm going to call the lab."

"Should we tell Croud?" Ray asked.

"Not yet. Let me call the lab and see if I can get hold of Shirley, or someone who can tell me what's going on."

Linda spent most of the morning calling and leaving messages at the police lab until someone picked up her call, and an irritated male voice told her—quite rudely, Linda thought—that somebody would get back to her when they had concluded all testing on the bones recovered from Sea Breeze Marina.

"What about the skull?" Linda persisted. "There was a skull with a gunshot wound, and the short report I got back today didn't mention it."

Linda heard the man at the other end of the call sigh heavily. "Wait a minute," he said curtly, and Linda could hear paper rustling and then the tapping sound of fingers on a keyboard. A few moments later, the man was back on the line.

"No skull documented here," he said. "Sorry, you must be mistaken."

"I'm not mistaken," Linda replied, exasperated. "I saw the skull myself."

"Are you sure? An untrained eye might mistake driftwood—"

"Shirley showed the skull to me. She pointed out the eye sockets. It had hair, and there was a gunshot wound." Linda was aware that her voice was getting louder, and any minute the man on the other end might drop the call, but she couldn't help it. With an enormous effort, she asked in a cajoling voice, "Please. I know you guys are really busy, but if you could look again? Or maybe put me through to Shirley? She hasn't returned my message yet."

"Oh, Shirley's on vacation," the man said. "And I've told you everything I know. You'll have to wait for the full report."

"Maybe the crime scene techs sent the skull somewhere else?" Linda was clutching at straws and also speaking to dead air. The man had ended the call. Then Linda realised what the man had said.

"Shirley's on vacation? That doesn't make sense," Linda said out loud.

"Everyone needs a holiday, Sarge," Ray said cheerfully. "You just had a couple of days off yourself."

"Yes, I know, Constable." Linda frowned at him, and then she told him what Shirley had said about taking vacation.

"And she specifically told me that the skull—"

"What skull?"

Staff Sergeant Croud was standing in the office doorway. "What skull?" he asked again.

"We were just looking over the report from the lab, sir," Linda said quickly, deciding not to tell him about the missing evidence yet. "They are still doing tests."

"So it's not a murder?" Croud asked. "I told you it was probably—"

"A homeless person, yes, sir, I remember. But there was a ring on one of the fingers, look."

Linda pointed to the murder board. "See? The ring looks good quality. It might not be a homeless person."

"A rich person then? Had too much to drink and then fell in the drink." Croud chuckled at his own pun.

"Shouldn't we at least start interviewing the liveaboards and other boaters at the marina? They might have heard or seen something, and somebody might recognise the ring.

Croud gave a noncommittal grunt. But it wasn't a no, so Linda continued, "Wouldn't cost much, sir, and look at it this way, if we can identify the victim, that would be a great result, right?"

"All right, all right. But not too much time. Not until we get something conclusive from the Grim—from the lab."

"So what are we going to ask them? We don't even know when the victim went in the water. He could be a visitor, or on holiday, and his family haven't missed him yet."

Linda and Ray sat opposite each other in the conference room. Linda was scribbling notes on a pad.

"We can ask if there are any boats that seem to be abandoned," she said, "and if someone hasn't paid for their moorage, I suppose. Then we can run down that lead. And we can ask them if they noticed anything weird. And there's the ring. It's quite distinctive."

"If anyone had seen someone fall in the water," Ray mused, "wouldn't they have mentioned that by now? And those bones could have been down there a while."

"Shirley didn't think he'd been down there that long. She said there were still bits of flesh on the bones. And the hair," Linda said, shuddering, remembering the wisp attached to the skull. "You've lived by the ocean all your life, haven't you?" she asked suddenly, a thought forming in her mind.

"Yep, Shell Bay born and bred." Ray nodded, taking a seat. "Have only been off the island five times," he added proudly. "One of those was for my RCMP training," he shuddered, "and the other four were to visit IKEA in Richmond."

"What? Why?"

"Everyone has to do their training, Sarge," he said, making a confused face.

"No, I meant why did you go to—never mind." Linda shook her head. "What I mean is, if you have lived by the ocean all your life, you know about crabs, right?"

"I know a lot about crabs, as it happens. Did you know if a crab crawls into a trap on its own, then it will just eat the bait and crawl out, but if other crabs are in there, if one crab tries to crawl out, the others will pull it back?"

"No, Ray, I did not know that. So, if a dead body is at the bottom of the ocean, how long would it take for crabs to pick it clean?"

"Ah, well, the Coast Guard in Saanich did a series of experiments on this with pigs," Ray said matter-of-factly. "They weighed them down on the ocean floor and filmed the whole process, at different depths."

Linda stared at Ray. "Did you go to some kind of forensic training to learn about that?" she asked, surprised at Ray's knowledge.

"No, Sarge. I was googling for barbecue pork recipes and I found it on YouTube."

"Ah, that makes sense now," Linda muttered. "So, how long did it take for the crabs to eat the dead pigs?"

"Couple of weeks, give or take," Ray said. "Quicker if the pigs were deeper because the sea lice helped. Why do you want to know?"

Linda closed her eyes. "Why do you think, Ray? I'm trying to figure out how long our victim was in the water before turning into a pile of bones. There was still flesh on the arm and other bones, and it's not very deep, and a man is bigger than a pig, so I'm thinking it can't be more than two weeks since our body was dumped in the ocean, right?"

"Good thinking, Sarge." Ray grinned at Linda. But then said, "So, how does that help us identify him, Sarge?"

"It doesn't, Ray, not specifically. But when we question people, we'll be able to narrow down the timeline to within two weeks. If anyone saw or heard something or any visitor who hasn't turned up to settle their bill. They should have records, and we might end up with a few names. And we can go through the missing persons records too.

Linda stood up suddenly, pushing her chair back and making Ray startle. "Right, come on, Constable. Enough sitting around. It's time to question the Wharf Rats. They know everything that goes on at the marina. We'll start there."

Chapter Fourteen.

It was nearly lunchtime when Ray and Linda arrived at the marina, and Ray practically jogged down the dock, eager, Linda presumed, to have lunch before starting on their task.

Croud had stopped them as they left the conference room, emphasising again that he didn't want them wasting time on a wild goose chase. "After all," he said, "that body could have been down there for ages. We might never know who it is."

Linda dragged Ray away before he launched into a long explanation of how quickly crabs can eat a pig's carcass, and had again reminded her boss that they were doing the right thing. "What if it turns out to be a murder, and we hadn't followed procedure?" she said, causing Croud's face to scrunch up as he seemed to wrestle internally with the conflict between budget overspend versus failure to follow correct police procedure. In the end, he turned and scurried back to his office, his head bobbing anxiously as he went.

"Ooh, darn it," Ray said, his hands on his hips. The sign on the Dine on the Dock Restaurant window said closed. He sniffed the air. "I can smell food," he said hopefully and pushed the restaurant door, but it was locked. "Never mind, Ray," Linda said impatiently. "Let's get a move on."

Beside the restaurant were two boathouses which swayed and bumped against the dock, and then a small floating office. It was brand new, spacious, and well-equipped.

After the murder of Commodore Hiscocks, there had been plenty of changes at Sea Breeze Marina. Joseph Jackson had been awarded the grant and permit to open Dine on the Dock where the old marina office used to be, and the City had also granted permission for a replacement office to be built for the new marina manager, Fiona Driver. Linda had met Fiona a few times and had decided she liked her. Fiona was a capable manager— efficient, friendly, and down-to-earth. Since Fiona had taken over the management of Sea Breeze Marina, the whole place was less tired and faded. Docks were repaired, boathouses had got fresh coats of paint, and best of all, Fiona had installed a state-of-the-art security system with cameras positioned all around the marina.

Just before they got to the office door, it was Linda's turn to sniff the air.

"Cigarette smoke?" Linda didn't think Fiona was a smoker, and just then a skinny lad with a mass of dark hair that obscured most of his face appeared from behind the office, cigarette in hand. He slouched along the deck, seemingly oblivious to his surroundings.

"Justin?"

Fiona stuck her head out of the office door and raised her voice at the boy who hastily tossed his cigarette into the ocean. He raised his head and stared at Fiona. "Yeah?" he mumbled.

"Don't do that," Fiona snapped. "Do you think visitors want to see your cigarette butts floating around?"

The boy dropped his head and muttered something through his mass of hair.

"Have you finished emptying the garbage cans yet?" Fiona asked. "No? Get on with it!"

Another lad materialised from the same direction. He was a little taller, but his hair was swept away from his face, and he walked with his shoulders back and his head up. There was the hint of a swagger in his walk and the tiniest smirk on his lips.

There was something about him that Linda recognised, but she couldn't put her finger on it. As he came nearer, Linda got a whiff of another smell. Something... fruity? This boy had been vaping, she realised. The cloying smell was worse than cigarettes. "Ah, Chad," Fiona called out. "Supervise Justin, would you? Make sure he's finished up with the rubbish."

"Yes, Mrs Driver," Chad answered and then nodded in Linda and Ray's direction. "It looks like you have visitors," he said.

Fiona turned her head and saw Ray and Linda. "Detective Sergeant? Constable? Do you have any news? You know, about the um... incident?" she asked anxiously, her voice lowering as if it was a secret.

Chad and Justin took advantage of the distraction to shuffle past Linda and Ray. Linda heard Ray grunt, and she looked up to see a scowl on his face. She wondered what the matter was but pushed that aside for later.

"Do you mind if we come in and have a word?" Linda asked, and Fiona nodded, gesturing for them to follow her into the small office.

Fiona pointed for them to sit down in two metal chairs in front of a desk. She slid behind the desk and took a seat. In front of her was a sandwich on a plate which oozed a little grease and smelled heavenly. Fiona smiled apologetically as she took a bite, and a shiny trickle dripped down her chin. "Sorry," she said, "I never have time for breakfast." Linda glanced at Ray. He was fixated on Fiona's food. She placed the half-eaten sandwich on her plate and shuffled paper to one side of her desk, then looked at them both.

"Do you have any news?" she asked again, as Linda fished into her pocket for her notebook and pen.

Before Linda could answer, Ray dragged his gaze away from Fiona's sandwich and asked, "Is that Chad Garner you've got working for you?"

Fiona looked a little startled at the question. "Yes. He's been working here for a while now. I'm very pleased with him. Why?"

"No reason," Ray muttered, but his face held the same dark expression he had when he saw the lad on the dock.

Garner. That was it. Linda now knew why the boy had seemed familiar. She arrested Ryan Garner, Chad's older brother, just a short while ago. Ryan, not the sharpest tool in the box, was fencing stolen goods, but not in a smart way. He had a posse of teenagers stealing children's bicycles for him, and he was then selling them on. The only problem for Ryan was that he was using social media for his sales and hadn't even bothered to use a fake account.

Constable Ray Reynolds, for reasons beyond Linda's comprehension, had known all about Ryan's Fagin-like enterprise, and instead of arresting him and all his teenage thieves, had merely issued a stern warning. Smarter people would have laid low for a bit, but not Ryan. He and his band of teenage thieves carried on swiping bicycles until Linda stepped in. It took two hours one evening for Linda to follow a kid who stole a bike which Linda had left leaned up against a garden wall on a quiet residential street. Obviously, the idiots had never heard of a decoy before. She took pictures of the kid stealing it, delivering it to Ryan, and then she waited until it appeared on Facebook. She messaged Ryan using a fake name and arranged to buy the bike the next day. As Ray led Ryan to the police cruiser, saying sorrowfully, "I'm disappointed in you, lad," Linda had caught sight of Chad watching his brother's downfall. And he had that very same smirk on his face now, she thought.

"Glad to hear it's going well," Linda said briskly, pushing thoughts of Chad Garner and his felon brother aside, and then informed Fiona of the reason for their visit.

"So you haven't identified the victim?" Fiona seemed perplexed. "Can't you use DNA tests or something? Or fingerprints… if there were any left?" she added with a shudder.

"DNA and fingerprints are only useful if we have something on file to run a comparison," Linda explained. "If the victim has never been in the police system, then these tests can't help."

"I see. Well, you can have access to my bookings if you want," Fiona said, "But I don't know how that will help. The summer visitors have all gone, everybody paid up when they left, and there are no boats left here that are unaccounted for. Our regular moorers come and go as they please during the day because the gate is unlocked, so we don't keep track."

"What about the liveaboards?" Linda asked.

"Ah, well, all of those are accounted for, I believe. Joseph, of course, is at the restaurant most days. I saw Sarah and Jewell yesterday. Then there's Alex Harding, a new young man who lives on The Lone Star. He's the new owner of the bookstore in town. And then there's Charles Harrington. Or Charles D. Harrington as he likes to be called. He's a writer and a bit pretentious. Although I haven't seen him for a while."

"Oh? He's missing?" Linda was instantly interested.

"Not missing as such. He often tucks himself away to write, I believe. The best person to ask is Jewell Winslow. They've become quite friendly. Very friendly, in fact." Fiona smiled. "Nice to see romance at that age."

Fiona waited while Linda scribbled in her notebook. "Anyone else?" Linda asked.

"There's Alison and Gary Binns." She gave a little tut.

Linda looked up from her scribbling. Fiona's face had darkened.

"Is there something you'd like to tell me about the Binns?" she asked.

Fiona sighed. "I don't like to gossip about people," she said. "The boating community is made up of all sorts of people, from all backgrounds, some rich, some poor…"

"Go on," Linda urged.

"Like I said, all kinds of backgrounds. But people on the water have a kind of camaraderie, Detective Sergeant. We help each other out when we can. But the Binns. They are most unpleasant, I'm afraid." She shrugged. "We can't all be friends, I suppose, but those two are rude and entitled."

"Do you know much about their background?" Linda asked.

"I think they are business owners of some kind," Fiona replied. "I really try not to spend any time with them."

"Okay," Linda wrote UNPLEASANT next to the names.

"Is there anything else?" Fiona asked.

"I'd like CCTV footage going back about two weeks," Linda said in the form of a statement, rather than a request. She hoped Fiona wouldn't ask her to get a court order because Linda was sure Croud wouldn't sanction it until it was officially confirmed they were investigating a murder. If she waited, she reasoned, the footage may be wiped.

"I'll get Chad on that," Fiona said to Linda's relief. "He's the techy one around here. I don't know how to work that stuff. Why two weeks? Do you think that's when the poor person went into the water?"

Ray answered before Linda could. "We think so. You see, it's all to do with the flesh left on the bones..." And he proceeded to describe the pig experiment to Fiona. When he'd finished, Fiona's face held an expression of disgust, and she stared at her sandwich for a second before pushing it away.

Bacon, Linda guessed.

"Was there anything else?" she asked.

"Just one last thing." Linda pulled out a photograph. She'd managed to crop the picture of the arm so that just the finger with the ring was displayed.

"Do you recognise this ring, or have any idea who it might belong to?"

Fiona leaned forward to look and then shook her head. "Sorry, not a clue."

Just then they heard a loud crash, and then clattering, interspersed with loud swear words.

Fiona sighed. "That's Joseph in the restaurant," she said. "He's particularly upset about the, um... discovery the other day. The restaurant might be closed for a while until this blows over. Apparently, there is a nasty rumor spreading around town that Joseph is serving up the very crab which may have... you know... eaten the body." The last words were said in a low voice as Fiona leaned towards Linda and Ray.

"I do hope this nasty business can be cleared up soon." She gestured at the paperwork on her desk. "I've already had cancellations for the rest of September, and our season ends in October. It's taken a long time to attract visitors and increase our revenue since the murder a few months ago. Now, after the arm was pulled up, we'll have to start again."

"Yes," Linda said dryly. "Murder is always very inconvenient. Especially for the victim."

"Oh no, do you think it was definitely murder?"

Linda backpedaled, mindful that this wasn't an official murder investigation yet.

"We are keeping an open mind," she said. "Thanks for your help. If you don't mind, we're going to be wandering around asking a few questions. But we'll be discreet."

"Thank you for that," Fiona said. "I'll get Chad working on the CCTV footage."

They all got up and moved out of the office.

Chad was waiting outside. Close enough, Linda thought, to have heard the entire conversation. Fiona explained to him about the CCTV footage.

"My pleasure," he said with a smirk. Linda understood why Ray disliked this little twerp.

Fiona turned to go back into her office.

"Oh, Mrs Driver?" Ray stopped her.

"Yes?"

"Were you going to finish that sandwich?"

Chapter Fifteen.

"Let's start with the Binns," Linda said as Ray emerged from Fiona's office once more with the leftover sandwich.

"Alright, Sarge," Ray said with his mouth full.

"Don't you ever stop eating?" "'Course," Ray said, sounding a little offended. "But look over there, Sarge."

Linda looked where Ray was pointing. Sarah Cooper was running towards them, waving her arms.

"Ray," Sarah said breathlessly. "Linda, we have information for you. About the body. We know who it is."

Sarah gestured for Linda and Ray to follow her to Jewell Winslow's boat. They both stepped onto the deck after Sarah.

"Jewell? The police are here," Sarah called out, and Linda heard what sounded like a muffled sob in reply.

"She's very upset," Sarah said in a low voice.

Linda and Ray squeezed into The Little Gem's small galley.

Jewell, who was pale with dark circles around her eyes, wordlessly handed Linda a photograph.

Sarah, who sat down next to Jewell at the galley table, explained the significance of the picture. "See the ring Charles is wearing? I am sure there was a ring on a finger of that... arm," Sarah's voice lowered, and she put her arm around Jewell's shoulder.

Linda pulled out the photograph of the arm at the lab and compared the two. "I'm sorry," she said, "It does appear to be the same. I understand that you and the victim were a couple?" she asked Jewell.

Jewell's face crumpled, and tears flowed down her face. "You called him a victim," she wailed, "I was hoping it was all a horrible mistake."

Linda waited until Jewell composed herself, and dried her eyes.

"We will have to do a DNA test," Linda explained gently. "But I'm afraid it does look like Charles Harrington is our... er... has died," she finished, changing her words hastily as Jewell seemed set to dissolve into tears once more.

She looked from Sarah to Jewell. There was something else, she realised. "Do you know what might have happened?"

Ray gave Linda a sideways glance, but Linda shook her head slightly. She didn't want to tell Sarah and Jewell about the skull. Not yet. She needed Shirley to sort her team out and get the proper report to them before she started sharing information. Rumours spread like wildfire in Shell Bay, and the last thing she needed, was the investigation to be compromised before it started.

"Well," Sarah started in a cautious tone, "There are some things you should know." She looked at Jewell, who nodded her head vigorously.

"Right then," Linda said, grabbing her notebook and pen, "you had better tell us."

Chapter Sixteen.

"What do you think, Sarge?"

"I don't know," Linda said slowly. "If it wasn't for the skull with the bullet hole, I would have said it was a lot of nonsense. More like some philanderer trying to wriggle out of an extramarital affair with some far-fetched story. I would have agreed with Jewell's first instincts. But now we have physical evidence."

"Why didn't you tell her about the skull?"

"Can't get ahead of the coroner's report, Constable," Linda answered briskly. "You know what Croud always says, we have to follow—"

"Proper procedure," Ray finished for her and grinned. "What about that manuscript she was talking about? Could Harrington really have been in fear for his life because of some book he was writing?"

"Jewell said it was something to do with local history." Linda shrugged. "I suppose if he was uncovering some scandal which might upset powerful people, it's possible. Can you think of any scandals in Shell Bay?"

Ray laughed. "We exposed them in the last case, Sarge. Merlin Melthorpe was the crime boss around here, and he's dead now. The only other scandal was the rigged talent contest."

"Oh, yes. The Neon Dreamers were a crime against pop music," Linda agreed. She checked the time.

"Let's interview Mr and Mrs Binns and finish for the day. We can do the rest when we've got the forensic report and we've checked out the CCTV. If Jewell did see something suspicious, it will be on there."

Detective Sergeant Linda Jenkins and Constable Ray Reynolds approached the pristine white yacht moored at the end of the dock away from The Little Gem, the Cosmos—which was Joseph's boat—and the Commodore, which was home for Sarah Cooper.

The Binns' yacht was a stark contrast to the weathered and worn boats that surrounded it. The Sea Breeze Marina was a hodgepodge of vessels, from modest sailboats to rustic houseboats, but this particular yacht stood out like a sore thumb, a symbol of wealth and privilege amidst the salt-of-the-earth charm of the marina.

As they made their way down the dock, Linda remembered what Fiona had told her about the Binns. She hoped they would be cooperative at least. It had been a long day.

Linda raised her hand and knocked on the side of the boat, the sound echoing hollowly across the water. For a long moment, there was no response. Then, just as she was about to knock again, a man appeared on the deck, an annoyed expression on his face.

He was tall and broad-shouldered, with a heavily tattooed neck and arms. His hair was slicked back, and he wore a sleeveless T-shirt. He looked out of place on the expensive yacht.

"Can I help you?" he asked, his tone clipped and impatient.

Linda held up her badge, her expression neutral. "Detective Sergeant Linda Jenkins and this is Constable Ray Reynolds. We're with the local police department. We're investigating a case and we were hoping to ask you a few questions."

The man's eyes narrowed, his gaze flicking between Linda and Ray. "A case? What kind of case?"

"I'm afraid there's been a discovery of human remains in the area," Linda said. "We're trying to gather information from everyone who may have seen or heard anything unusual in the past few weeks."

The man's eyes widened, and he arched his eyebrows. Linda thought he almost looked amused. "Human remains?" he said. "You mean, like a dead body?"

Linda nodded. "Yes, sir. Exactly like that. Can we come aboard, please, and ask you and your wife a few questions? It won't take long."

"I suppose." The man shrugged, his expression bored. "Can't see how we can help you. We keep ourselves to ourselves." He gestured for Linda and Ray to step onto the deck. "In there," he said and pointed to the cabin. "My wife is up in the wheelhouse. I'll get her. Make yourselves at home."

The cabin was spacious, far larger than The Little Gem or any of the boats that Linda had been on. It was fitted with a full kitchen, complete with granite countertops.

There was room for a couch and two easy chairs, and in a small nook, there was a computer desk. A laptop was open. Linda moved over and nudged the desk.

"What are you doing, Sarge?" Ray said in a loud whisper.

"Nothing."

The movement made the laptop screen come to life, but all Linda could see was a logo, some kind of nautical theme she thought, before Gary came back into the cabin and she casually moved away from the desk.

Just then, a woman appeared behind Gary, her blonde hair perfectly swept into a messy bun and her makeup flawless. She was dressed in a designer sundress and high heels, looking more like she was ready for a fashion shoot than a day at the marina.

She stepped into the cabin and glared at Linda and Ray. "Who are these people, Gary?" she asked, her voice high-pitched and nasal. "What do they want?"

Gary sighed, rolling his eyes. "They're cops, Alison. They're investigating some kind of case. A dead body or something."

Alison's eyes widened, her hand flying to her mouth. "A dead body? Oh my God, that's horrible. I can't believe they'd let something like that happen here. This place is such a dump."

"Ma'am, I assure you that we're doing everything we can to investigate this case," Linda said, keeping her voice even. "Can I start with your names first?" Linda pulled out her notebook and pen.

The man hesitated for a moment as if debating whether to answer. Then, with a sigh, he said, "Gary. Gary Binns."

"And?" Linda turned to his wife, although she'd heard Gary call her by name a moment earlier.

"Alison Binns," she snapped. "I'm his wife and business partner."

"And your business is..."

"None of yours," Alison replied, but Gary held up his hand and shot his wife a warning glance.

"Be nice, babe," he said. "They're just doing their job." And then to Linda, he added, "Salvage and waste management."

Linda wrote that down. "Appropriate surname, sir," she said brightly.

Gary Binns grinned. "My name used to be Biggs, but I changed it—legally—to Binns when I started the business."

"Can we get on with this?" Alison cut in.

"Yes, of course. Can you tell us if you've noticed anything unusual or suspicious in the past few weeks?"

Alison shrugged, her expression bored. "Not really. I mean, we don't really pay attention to what goes on around here. We just come here to get away from it all, you know? To relax and enjoy ourselves."

Linda nodded, making another note in her notebook. She could tell that getting any useful information out of this couple was going to be like pulling teeth.

"You're sure?"

"Yes, we're sure," the wife replied.

"Do you spend any time with the rest of the community here? Eat at the restaurant at all?"

"Absolutely not," Alison said. "We stay on our boat and order in. I don't know any of the... er... other people here. Except for Fiona, the manager, and her assistant, Chad."

Linda heard Ray snort when he heard Chad's name.

"Well, thank you for your time," she said, snapping her notebook shut. "If you think of anything that you think might help, please don't hesitate to contact us. We'll be in touch if we have any further questions."

Gary nodded, his expression dismissive. "Yeah, sure. Whatever you say, Detective."

"Well, that was a waste of time," Ray muttered, shaking his head when they were walking away from the Binns' yacht. "Those two don't know anything. And even if they did, they wouldn't tell us. Too busy looking down their noses at everyone else."

Linda sighed, running a hand through her hair. "I know. But we had to interview them. Proper procedure."

She glanced back at the yacht over her shoulder. "I know why Fiona doesn't like them. There's something about them that doesn't sit right with me. The way they talked about the marina, the way they dismissed everyone who lives here... It's like they think they're better than everyone else, just because they have money and a fancy boat."

Ray nodded. "Yeah, I got that feeling too. And did you see the way Alison was looking at Gary? Like he was a meal ticket, not a husband. I bet she's only with him for the money."

They passed Fiona on the way out.

"Chad will drop off the CCTV footage," she called out. "Let me know if you need any more help."

"At least we have the identity of our victim," Linda said as they drove back to the detachment. "That ring really helped. So we've made progress, Constable."

"We have, Sarge," Ray agreed. "Not a bad day at all."

Chapter Seventeen.

Chad had watched Constable Ray Reynolds leave the marina with that stuck-up detective, or sergeant, or whatever she was, and chuckled to himself. Deputy Doofus was what he and Ryan, his older brother, used to call Reynolds. What an idiot. All those times Reynolds had visited Ryan and given him one of his 'chats' about keeping on the straight and narrow, blah, blah, and blah, and all the while, there were stolen bikes, TVs, and laptops all around the house, right under Reynolds' nose.

He thought Ryan was just selling stolen bikes, but you name it, Ryan and Chad nicked it. Except they were too smart to do the actual nicking.

It had been Ryan's idea to use the local kids. Get them to scout out neighborhoods with lots of families, check out the front yards or driveways where kids always dump their bikes, and then come back later and swipe them. After all, who would stop a kid with a bike? The kids all got a fair cut. Then Ryan sold them on.

But then Ryan got lazy. Instead of making deals himself, he just put the stolen bikes on eBay or Facebook Marketplace. He got complacent, and of course, he was going to get caught. Deputy Doofus had taken his time to catch on to Ryan's scheme and had even given him a second chance, but Ryan had continued being sloppy until he'd been caught again. And this time, it was that mean Detective Sergeant Jenkins who'd arrested him. Chad's stupid big brother was now waiting for his court date.

Chad sighed to himself. Ryan wasn't exactly a criminal mastermind.

When Ryan was led away in handcuffs, humiliated by Deputy Doofus, Chad had made a promise to himself to never, ever let that happen to him. He would do better than Ryan. Chad was smart. He would study all the famous gangsters and even the local ones. The great criminals were the ones who learned from the mistakes of others. Being flashy with your cash was a huge mistake, as Ryan was apt to do occasionally. Being a big mouth and attracting attention was also a rookie error. Ryan often boasted about how much cash he was making and how dumb the police were. Chad would do everything differently.

Merlin Melthorpe had been Shell Bay's most notorious criminal. He was a founding member of the biker gang, The Vipers, and he had built an empire of organised crime until he was finally taken down during a shootout at the Big Beefy Burger joint. Melthorpe had gone to prison, and when he got out, he'd been murdered.

The loss of Merlin Melthorpe had left a void in Shell Bay's criminal underworld. And that had given Chad all the inspiration he needed. The void needed filling. And Chad Garner was the man to do it.

The first obstacle he had was to make sure that Big Normy, Melthorpe's muscle and right-hand man, was out of the game. Big Normy, by all accounts, had been broken up when Melthorpe was killed. Melthorpe had left his house to Big Normy, but apparently, the big man couldn't bring himself to live in the place where his beloved boss had met his grisly end and was living in a trailer in the backyard.

Chad had pondered what to do. He didn't want to work hard at building a well-oiled criminal enterprise, only to find himself in a turf war with Big

Normy. It would be a waste of time and resources. Negotiation was key, Chad decided. Mafia families did it all the time. The bosses would meet, hash out their differences, agree on who was in charge of what, and ensure that no blood would be shed.

Chad had borrowed Ryan's old leather jacket to make himself appear tougher, and one Sunday morning, he'd visited Big Normy.

When he rapped on the trailer door, it took a few moments for a response. Then the trailer swayed a little, as if someone was moving, and Chad could hear a muffled voice before the flimsy door was pulled open, and Big Normy barked out, "Who the hell are you?"

Big Normy towered over Chad. To be fair, he was standing on the top step of the trailer, but even so, Chad hadn't realised that Big Normy was, in fact, big. He had big arms, big hands, and, Chad noted, a big stomach that hung over his belt buckle, which was also big. He also didn't have a very friendly expression on his face.

Chad had a moment when he thought that approaching Big Normy with his proposal for dividing up Shell Bay's crime patch might not be a good idea, but Big Normy was glowering at him. "Well?" he growled again. "Who are you, and what do you want?"

"I'm Chad Garner," Chad started and then outlined his plan, which was very fair, in his opinion.

Five minutes later, Chad was rubbing his backside, which had taken quite a hefty kick from Big Normy. Even in his socks, Big Normy had put some considerable force behind it, and there was bound to be a bruise. Safe to say that the meeting hadn't gone as Chad planned. Big Normy threatened to break his 'scrawny neck' if Chad ever bothered him again. On the bright side, Big Normy hadn't specifically told him not to start up his own criminal organisation, had he? Chad decided to take the win.

What Chad needed now was an opportunity he could transform into a workable business model. He needed to keep a low profile, follow instructions, and even put up with being ordered to pick up garbage by Mrs Driver. This job was a necessary part of building his own successful gangster career. In fact, working at the marina had worked out better than he first thought.

Chad had only taken the summer job because his mother had been all freaked out when Ryan was arrested. "I won't have both my boys in trouble with the law," she'd declared. "You get yourself a job and stay on the straight and narrow." The only job he could find was the marina assistant, and that was only because Fiona Driver didn't know who he was. Everyone else in Shell Bay knew he was Ryan's brother, and he was effectively blacklisted.

He soon found out that marina assistant meant marina dogsbody. Cleaning up otter poop, emptying the bins, and cleaning toilets were part of the daily routine, Fiona had explained. When you've proved you can keep the marina shipshape, you can graduate to making reservations and taking payments from the guests. Chad smiled and said all the right things—that he was here to work hard and learn everything he could—and Fiona had nodded approvingly.

In a short space of time, Chad had gained Fiona Driver's trust. It had been Chad who'd proposed a new security system. "CCTV cameras," he had explained to Fiona. "Everyone will feel safer. It will be much appreciated by our valued guests, and you might get a discount on the insurance."

Fiona appeared impressed. "Great initiative," she said and had allowed Chad to pick the system, install it, and be the primary contact. Chad couldn't believe how easy it had been. On his very own cell phone, he commanded power over the cameras. He could turn them on or off at will, point them in different directions, and even download and edit the footage. Every evening, after Fiona and that dumb idiot Justin left, he could wander the marina at will and poke around in boathouses and storage sheds. He could spy on boat owners, practice his surveillance techniques, and collect intel which might be useful. It would have been easy to pilfer here and there from empty boats. Valuables were always left lying on decks.

But Chad wasn't like Ryan. He didn't want to be a petty thief. He wanted a career. An empire. And so he'd pick up their belongings and leave a note for the owners to collect them at the marina office. The boaters were always grateful and Chad was building a reputation for being honest and trustworthy.

He grinned to himself and sucked on his vape, then exhaled the strawberry-scented smoke. When he had finally masterminded his criminal enterprise, Chad Garner would be beyond suspicion. Even Big Normy would be impressed.

Chapter Eighteen.

The next morning, Linda and Ray got an early start.

Under the victim column on the murder board, Linda wrote, Charles D. Harrington.

"So we have our victim, Constable. The crime scene guys will confirm it once they've got a DNA sample off his boat. So, what do we know about Charles D. Harrington? And why would somebody want to kill him?"

Ray glanced up at Linda. She noticed his look. "Ray, I saw the skull with the gunshot hole in it. He was murdered. I am certain there was just a mix-up at the lab. You'll see."

"Do you believe Jewell's story about a secret manuscript, Sarge? And the mysterious people on the boat?"

Linda shrugged. "I don't know, Ray. It seems a bit far-fetched. But I asked the forensic guys to have a look around Harrington's boat to see if they can find it. And they will swab for fingerprints. Oh, and we can check the CCTV to see if Jewell's story about strange people on the dock checks out. In the meantime, we'll find out everything we can about the victim. So, what have you got so far?"

Linda walked over to stand behind Ray as he turned to the computer they had set up in the conference room. She peered at the screen over his shoulder while he fumbled with his mouse.

"Ray, what are you doing? I didn't ask you to look up Chad Garner."

A red stain rose up Ray's neck. "He's trouble," Ray muttered. "I wouldn't be surprised if he was mixed up in all this."

"Mixed up in what, Ray? We don't even know for sure that it's a murder yet. And if it is, do you think that scrawny kid could have done it?"

Ray shrugged. "He could have, I reckon," he said defensively.

"Ray, he did seem like an objectionable little..." Linda struggled for a suitable description that wasn't a cuss word but gave up. "Whatever he is, he hasn't—as yet—committed a crime as far as we know. And you gave his brother a break, remember? Why do you dislike Chad so much?"

"He's just a... he's just a cocky little... he called me Deputy Doofus," Ray muttered.

"Okay, can we get back to real police work, Ray? Instead of persecuting innocent kids because they called you rude names?"

Linda pulled a chair over to the desk. "Move over. Let's search for Charles D. Harrington."

Ray hastily started typing into the police database. They waited while the icon in the middle of the screen circled and circled, and then the search came back: No search items found.

"Try without the D," Linda said. "People sometimes do that to sound more important or something. And writers can be a bit pretentious."

That search didn't return anything either.

"Not in the database then. Let's try social media and Google."

Ray dutifully typed away, and a few minutes later, they still had nothing.

"That's odd," Linda said. "No online presence at all. Jewell said he had a publisher, although she didn't know the titles of the books he's published."

"Pen name?" guessed Ray.

"Could be. Or Charles D. Harrington is his pen name, and his real name is something else. But no Facebook account. Hmmm." Linda thought for a moment, then pulled out her phone.

"Jewell is on Instagram," she said, "Maybe she took a picture of Charles and tagged him." She found the account and scrolled through the photos. "Nothing. Just sunsets and artsy stuff."

Both Linda and Ray lapsed into silence. Where else could they find anything about Charles D. Harrington? All they had was a photograph and a pile of bones.

"Hang on a minute," Linda said, and she grabbed her phone and dug in her pocket for the business card she'd taken from Fiona's desk. She tapped in Fiona's number and waited.

"Hi, Fiona? It's Detective Sergeant Linda Jenkins here. Sorry to bother you, but I wondered if you have credit card details on file for Charles Harrington."

She waited a minute. "No? He paid with cash. Did he give you any ID? Anything with an address? No? Right."

Ray started flapping his hand in front of her and mouthing something. "What? No, sorry, not you, Fiona."

"Boat registration, Sarge," Ray said excitedly, "Get the boat name, and we can search the registration."

"Great idea!" Linda grinned, "Did you hear that, Fiona? We need the boat name."

A few moments later, "What did you say? Oh, of course it's something like that," Linda rolled her eyes and scribbled a note down on a piece of scrap paper on Ray's desk.

When she ended the call, she showed Ray. "Scribbler's Solace. I might have known it would be a dumb name like that."

Ray looked puzzled. "Scribbler's what? I don't get it."

"Writers? Scribblers? You see?"

Ray looked blank.

"Never mind. It was a great idea to trace the boat. See if you can get somewhere with this."

Linda left Ray looking up the boat registry and went back to her desk. She checked her email. Still nothing from the lab, and no emails or messages from Shirley either.

Maybe she should leave another message. She called her, but this time, it rang out; the call didn't even connect to voicemail.

This was all so strange. A skull with a gunshot wound that was now missing, a coroner who had gone on holiday for maybe the first time in her career, and a murdered boater or writer who didn't seem to exist apart from one photograph and a ring on an unidentified arm. Add to that Jewell's story about the manuscript...

Linda doodled absently on a pad of paper in front of her. One thing she did know was that Sarah Cooper and Jewell Winslow were convinced Harrington was murdered. She hoped they weren't going to play detectives again. The last time Sarah did that, she'd nearly died.

Linda massaged her forehead. There was only one thing to do—get back to basic policing. She looked at her notes from earlier in the day. Ray was chasing down Charles Harrington's boat; she might as well check out the other liveaboards. Especially the Binns. She was just typing Gary Binns' name into the police database when Ray appeared at her desk.

"Well?" she looked up, hoping he'd found something. He held a piece of paper in his hand.

"The boat is owned by a corporation. I just printed out the details," he said, putting the document in front of her. "See? It's just a numbered company, but it is registered in British Columbia, so I've requested more details from the BC Companies Registry. I won't get it until tomorrow, though."

Linda nodded. "Maybe Charles Harrington was a director or something. Good work, Ray."

Ray smiled before he turned to go back to his desk just as Linda had a thought. "Ray? Why don't you check the boat registry for the Binn's boat? What was it called again? The Godfather or something?"

"The Goodfella," Ray said with a grin. "I'm telling you, Sarge, that Gary Binns was giving off gangster vibes."

"Constable, vibes are not evidence," Linda said briskly, although she secretly agreed with him. "But run the boat through the registry and see what you get. And then I'm checking them in the database right now."

Linda pressed *Enter* and let the program sort through all its data until seconds later, it brought up a result.

"Hello, what do we have here?" Linda murmured and inwardly groaned. Could Ray possibly be right about Gary Binns? If he was, she'd never hear the end of it.

She quickly scanned his file and saw that Gary Binns had legally changed his name five years ago like he said he had. But what he failed to mention was that, as Gary Biggs, he had an impressive list of convictions. Most of them were petty crimes—shoplifting, theft, breaking and entering—but nothing violent, and he had managed to stay out of prison. Since Gary had become a Binns rather than a Biggs, he had a clean record.

There was nothing gangster-like in his file, Linda noted with relief. Gary Binns was just one of those macho guys who liked to project a hard man image. And the play on the cliche of waste management and organised crime was just an advertising ploy, she decided. The vulgar gold chains, the tattoos, and the ostentatious display of wealth just further enhanced that image.

Certainly, Gary Binns was doing much better than Gary Biggs. There was nothing on record about Alison Binns at all, except she was listed as Gary's spouse and business partner.

Linda was beginning to think that this was all a waste of time. So what if they couldn't find anything about Charles D. Harrington? Maybe he was just a married guy who had taken a shine to Jewell Winslow and then didn't have the guts to come clean about his wife. He'd just left a mysterious note to make Jewell think he was this exciting shadowy figure, instead of a philandering, deceitful man. Jewell had even suspected as much to start with. Maybe her instincts were right.

Poor Jewell. Linda could sympathise. She'd been the 'other woman', and all she'd been left with was a broken heart and shame. But if their dead victim was married, there was no trace of it at all.

She consulted her notes again. She might as well run Alex Harding through the database, and then there was nothing else she could do until the final report came in from Shirley's office.

She was just typing the name when Croud called out. "Detective Sergeant Jenkins? My office. Now, please."

Linda deleted her search and got up from her desk. She grabbed her notebook. Maybe Shirley's team had finally found the missing evidence, and she could really get her teeth into a new murder investigation.

Chapter Nineteen.

L inda knocked and entered Staff Sergeant Croud's office. She was surprised to see Mayor Godson already sitting in a chair.

"Sir, you wanted to see me?"

"Sit down, Jenkins. Yes, I've got good news." He beamed. "It's excellent news for all of us."

Linda wasn't sure what to think. "What news is that, sir?"

Croud waved a piece of paper at her. "No murder. It says right here."

Linda felt anger rising, and her face getting hot. "I'm sorry, Staff Sergeant," Linda said, her voice tight with barely contained frustration. "But I wasn't aware that you had received a forensic report, let alone shared it with the mayor."

She shot Mayor Godson a stern look, and he seemed to wilt under her gaze.

"This is not proper procedure, sir."

Staff Sergeant Croud's smile faltered slightly, seeming to sense the tension in Linda's tone. "Well, Detective Sergeant, I thought it was important to keep the mayor informed, given the high-profile nature of the case."

Linda's eyes narrowed, her suspicion growing by the second. "With all due respect, Staff Sergeant, I should have been the first to know about any developments in the case. And frankly, I find it hard to believe that the forensic evidence suddenly points away from murder."

Mayor Godson's brow furrowed. "What do you mean, Detective? The report clearly states that the remains show no signs of foul play. Do you disagree?"

"It doesn't matter if the Detective Sergeant agrees or not, mayor," Croud snapped. "It's not up to her. It's up to the Coroner's office, and they say, on this very report," he shook the piece of paper again, "that it was an accidental death, not murder. So no expensive investigating. And that's that."

"But sir, I told you..."

"But nothing, Detective Sergeant..."

"Wait a minute, Croud," the mayor interrupted. "Detective Sergeant Linda Jenkins is a hero in this town. I'd like to hear what she has to say."

Linda and Croud looked at the mayor, confused. Linda recovered quickly.

"I don't think," she said carefully, "that all the evidence has been examined. That's all. I'd like the coroner's office and the forensic lab to take another look, to see if they missed anything."

Croud glared at her.

"Well, that seems perfectly reasonable," Mayor Godson said, rubbing his hands together. "So we might well have another murder on our hands then."

"Wait a minute," Croud said. "I thought you would be glad it isn't another murder, what with all the publicity over the last one?"

"Well, obviously, I hope we don't have another murderer running around Shell Bay," Mayor Godson said. "But on the other hand, we did see a rise in tourism this summer."

"What?" Croud and Linda said together, both in tones of disbelief.

"And the thing is, that damn true crime podcast everyone is listening to, it's going on and on about the last murder, and it's time the town got some closure and moved on to something else..."

"Wait a minute," Linda interrupted. "So you are hoping for a new murder to take everyone's mind off the last one?"

"Exactly." The mayor beamed. "Righto, Croud. See you tomorrow for the press conference."

As Linda and Croud watched the mayor leave the office in stunned silence, Ray put his head around the door.

"Sorry to interrupt, Sarge," he said. "The forensics from Harrington's boat match the bones. So Harrington is definitely our victim."

"Thanks, Ray. Did they find a manuscript or anything else?"

Ray shook his head. "No, Sarge."

Linda was disappointed.

"What's this about a manuscript?" Croud demanded.

Linda told him briefly about her interview with Jewell and Sarah.

Croud waved his hand dismissively when she was finished. "Sounds like a lot of hysterical nonsense. I'm surprised at you, Jenkins, listening to a lot of gossip from the Wharf Rats at the marina. This," he picked up the report again, "is evidence. Right here."

"But sir, it's not all the evidence, is it?" Linda argued. "What about the skull?"

"There was no skull," Croud said in exasperation, "You were mistaken. It's not like the lab to misplace evidence, is it?"

"What if they didn't misplace it?" Linda insisted. "It's very convenient that the only other person who can confirm its existence has gone on vacation for the first time in her life."

Staff Sergeant Croud's face paled. "Detective Sergeant Jenkins, are you suggesting that the forensic report has been tampered with?"

Linda met his gaze. "I'm not suggesting anything, Staff Sergeant. I'm stating a fact. Something stinks here, and it's not just the remains we found."

"That's ridiculous," Croud declared, but with less energy. "Jenkins, I'm giving a press conference tomorrow morning with the mayor. And I'm telling the good people of Shell Bay that we have no evidence of murder. Is that clear?"

Linda was silent.

"Is that clear, Jenkins?" Croud repeated with more force.

"Yes, sir."

Chapter Twenty.

Sarah and Jewell watched as, once again, crime scene technicians dressed head to toe in their white overalls descended on Sea Breeze Marina.

They were searching Charles' sailboat, The Scribbler's Solace. Sarah thought it was a pretentious name for a boat. But also, if Charles D. Harrington was paranoid, why choose a name for a boat that stood out?

She hoped the sight of the forensic team wouldn't upset Jewell again, but her friend had remained stony-faced as the technicians crawled all over the boat.

It was all over in a few hours.

Fiona Driver had been very kind to Jewell, asking if she needed anything. Chad, one of the maintenance lads, was hovering about, trying to ask the technicians questions.

"Bugger off," one of them told him. "None of your business."

It didn't seem to deter Chad at all, who just watched from a distance, puffing on his sickly-smelling vape, until Fiona told him to do some work.

Gary Binns leaned lazily on the rail of his yacht, obviously also curious about the goings-on.

"I thought this was a quiet marina," he called to Fiona, who rolled her eyes. "We should get a discount for all the disruption."

"It doesn't seem right," Jewell muttered. "Charles was so private."

"It will be over soon," Sarah said. "And it is necessary, Jewell. You want to find out what happened to Charles, don't you?"

Jewell nodded. "I suppose," she said. "Although nothing will bring him back, will it?"

Later that evening, Sarah, Jewell, and Joseph sat on the deck of The Little Gem. Sarah and Joseph brought wine and food to share with Jewell, who hadn't had the energy to cook. They were all subdued as the evening turned into a clear September night.

Linda had called earlier. It was definitely Charles, she'd said. The forensic team had matched his DNA to the bones. But their search had not turned up other evidence.

"No manuscript," she'd told Sarah, and then explained that a press conference was scheduled for the following day.

"What now?" Sarah had asked. "Will there be an investigation?"

"I'm sorry," Linda had said. "I can't say." And she'd ended the call before Sarah could ask her any more questions.

"I had to close the restaurant," Joseph explained, grumpily. "Until all this business is over."

"Joseph." Sarah gave him a warning glance.

"Sorry, Jewell," he said hastily. "I didn't mean..."

"It's okay," she said and lapsed back into silence.

The marina was quiet. Fiona left for the day, and Justin had shuffled after her, grunting his goodbyes to us all. Sarah wondered briefly where Chad was. He was a strange boy and made her feel slightly uneasy.

She thought about her conversation with Linda.

"I'll go to the press conference tomorrow," she said. "If you'd like. They will probably announce the murder investigation."

"Are they sure it's murder?" Joseph asked, surprised.

Sarah realised that Joseph didn't know about the manuscript or the unidentified people at the marina or on Charles' boat.

She told him the whole story.

"Another murder," he said, shaking his head. "I thought we were done with all that. And how did anyone get into the marina? I thought we had a proper security system. That Chad was supposed to be the whiz kid with all that technology."

Just then, they heard shuffling, as if someone was moving around the dock. Followed by a small sound that sounded like a cough.

Joseph stood up. "Anyone there?" he called. There was silence.

"Probably just an otter," he said as he sat down again. "So tell me more about this manuscript. If it wasn't on Charles' boat, where could it be?"

Chapter Twenty-One

C had shrunk back into the shadows.

That was close. Time to go, he reasoned. He didn't want to get caught snooping around.

He waited until he heard voices again, then moved silently along the dock, avoiding the pools of light that spilled between the boats from the full moon rising above the marina.

He was about to make the turn from the office to go up the ramp when someone gripped his shoulder and yanked him. Chad would have let out an involuntary squeal, but a hand clamped over his mouth.

Chad was dragged backwards into the boathouse beside the closed restaurant.

"Listen to me, you little rat," a man's voice growled in his ear. "I've been watching you, snooping around, poking your nose into other people's business."

Chad tried to speak, but the hand over his mouth tightened.

The voice sounded amused. "I've got you, little rat. I know all about you and your stupid brother, Ryan. I know you've been turning off the security system and rigging the cameras. One phone call to the police, and they'll be looking at you for this murder."

Chad squeaked with fear and tried to shake his head.

"But I've got a proposition for you," the voice continued. "New employment. You now work for me, you hear?"

Chad tried to shake himself free.

"Do you understand? Because if you don't, then you'll either be going down for murder... or down to the bottom of the ocean."

Chad stopped struggling. He was aware that he had peed his pants. His chest was hurting as he tried to fill his lungs with air, as the man's hand was partially over his nose.

"Now, I'll ask again, do you understand? You work for me, right?"

This time, Chad nodded. The man whispered instructions. Chad listened through the sound of blood pounding in his ears, his fear causing him to tremble uncontrollably.

"I'm going to let you go now, little rat," the man said, once he'd finished relaying his instructions, his lips so close to Chad's ear that they brushed against his skin. "You are going to run up the ramp and go home without looking back."

With that, Chad was free. He gasped for breath and then did exactly what he was told. He ran up the ramp and out of the marina. It wasn't until he was in the parking lot and was sure he wasn't being followed that he stopped and looked back at the boathouse. There was no sign of anyone in the shadows, just the gentle movement as it rocked on the tide.

Chapter Twenty-Two.

The next morning, just before the press conference was about to begin, Linda arrived at City Hall. She parked her car and made her way to the front entrance, where reporters and photographers from local media outlets were already filing in. She followed them, waving her badge at the mayor's assistant, Karen, who looked as irritated by the whole event as Linda was.

Linda stood with her arms crossed, not bothering to hide her irritation. She hated press conferences, mainly because she despised journalists who were, in her opinion, a bunch of immoral hyenas. This morning, she doubly hated being at a press conference because Croud was about to give a bunch of misleading information.

In Linda's experience, it was best to give the press nothing than something incorrect, because when they found out, reporters loved nothing more than a story that made the police look like bungling idiots. And Linda was certain that the missing skull would eventually be found, and then they would all have to backtrack and tell Shell Bay that they had been wrong, and there was, in fact, a killer running around the community again.

That thought made Linda wonder about Agnes, who also considered the police to be a bunch of bungling idiots and never passed up an opportunity to tell Linda.

The previous night, Agnes was not prowling around when Linda parked the car outside her apartment. The main house had been in darkness, which Linda thought was a little odd. Agnes was a night owl. She was also up early. In fact, Linda wasn't sure if the woman ever slept at all. She supposed that was the only way Agnes kept on top of all the goings-on in Shell Bay.

She had wondered for a moment if she should knock on the door to check if Agnes was okay, but decided against it. She didn't have the energy for one of Agnes' interrogations.

Instead, Linda had gone inside and surveyed the contents of her fridge, which was pitiful. She ended up finishing a bottle of white wine Joanna had left and eating a lump of cheese, after scraping off the grey fuzz from one end and the dried, cracked bit from the other.

Then she had pulled her clothes off and fallen into bed, and a dreamless sleep as soon as her head hit the pillow.

This morning, there was no sign of Agnes either.

When Linda had arrived at the office, she'd found Ray Reynolds already there, his cell phone to his ear. She assumed it was a personal call because he hurriedly ended the conversation. "Croud wants us at the press conference," he told Linda.

So here they both were, waiting for the debacle to begin, Linda thought as she scanned the crowd. She spied Sarah Cooper standing at the back of the conference room, waiting for the presser to begin. She wasn't surprised to see her. She had called to tell Sarah and Jewell about the press conference.

Finally, Staff Sergeant Croud and Mayor Godson walked in and stood in front of the microphone facing the small crowd of journalists. Croud had a smug expression on his face. He was convinced he was right about this, and Linda had heard him gushing on the phone earlier to his superior.

"Oh yes, sir. I knew it wasn't a murder, of course, but we had to dot every I and cross every T, follow the proper procedure... yes, right you are, sir. I'll make sure the press are fully informed..."

The mayor, in contrast, looked agitated. Linda was not surprised. The press had been merciless in their attacks about his pop star career.

Neon Nightmare! Lead singer is a fraud, screamed one headline. *Mayor, couldn't hold a tune in a bucket*, was another. Linda had been surprised when Mayor Godson had insisted on doing this joint press conference with Croud, as he had kept himself out of the public eye since the Hiscocks case.

The reporters were surprised to see him too, judging by the murmur that had gone through the crowd when Mayor Godson stepped up to join Croud behind the podium. The room was buzzing with anticipation, as the local reporters held their phones, ready to record the statement, and there were a couple of photographers fiddling with their equipment, waiting for Croud to start.

Croud spoke, his voice steady and authoritative. "Good morning, everyone. Thank you for coming today. Mayor Godson and I have called this press conference to share some important updates regarding the recent discovery of human remains at the Sea Breeze Marina."

The room fell silent with only the sound of the soft clicking of cameras and the occasional shuffle of feet. Croud cleared his throat, his gaze sweeping over the assembled journalists.

"After a thorough investigation and analysis of the forensic evidence, we can now confidently state that the unidentified body parts found at the marina were not, in fact, the result of foul play."

A murmur rippled through the crowd as the reporters exchanged surprised words. Croud continued, his voice rising slightly to be heard over the growing chatter.

"Our team of experts has determined that the remains were likely the result of a tragic accident or natural causes. While we will continue to investigate the circumstances surrounding this incident, we want to assure the public that there is no ongoing threat to the safety of our community."

He turned to the mayor. "Mayor Godson, do you have anything to add?"

Mayor Godson nodded solemnly, his hands clasped in front of him. "We understand that this has been a difficult and unsettling time for the people of Shell Bay. But rest assured, your local law enforcement and government officials are working tirelessly to bring closure to this case and to ensure the well-being of our town."

Croud was nodding along, his face grave.

The mayor continued. "And while we respect the forensic findings, we continue to urge our law enforcement to keep an open mind, because as the good folks of Shell Bay know, there is nothing worse than living with the threat of a killer in our midst."

Croud's head snapped around as if he were the victim of whiplash, and he glared at the mayor before elbowing his way in front of the microphone again.

"Except that in this case, we are certain that there was no murder and everyone is safe, so no need to worry. Everything is under control. So, any questions?"

A young reporter near the front of the room raised her hand. "Staff Sergeant Croud, can you explain the apparent gunshot wound to the skull that was found by divers? It was reported by sources close to the investigation."

Linda nearly gasped out loud. How the hell had they found out?

Croud's eyes widened, his face reddening as he struggled to maintain his composure. "I'm sorry, but I'm not aware of any gunshot wound. Our forensic team has thoroughly examined the remains and found no evidence of foul play."

The reporter pressed on, undeterred. "But our sources indicate that there was a clear bullet hole in the skull fragment recovered at the scene.

How do you reconcile that with your statement about the lack of foul play?"

Croud's jaw clenched, his anger rising at the unexpected line of questioning. He glanced at Mayor Godson, who looked equally taken aback by the journalist's assertion.

Before Croud could formulate a response, another reporter chimed in. "Staff Sergeant, have you heard the latest episode of the Death on the Dock podcast? They've been covering this case extensively and have raised some serious questions about the handling of the investigation."

Croud's face paled, his eyes darting around the room as if he were looking for an escape route.

Just then, Linda heard a loud beeping sound. And then another, and another. For a moment, the room went quiet as the journalists checked their phones.

Croud gestured to the mayor that they should leave, and the two men took a couple of steps towards the door. Before they both reached safety, one reporter shouted, "Staff Sergeant Croud. What can you tell us about a missing manuscript? Is that why the victim was killed?"

Croud swung around, his face flushed with rage. "Where the hell did you get..."

"So you're not denying it? It's definitely murder?" the reporter pressed, as Croud's head started bobbing frantically. "And do you have any comments about the Shadowcaster's Death on the Dock podcast?"

Linda covered her face. The damn podcast. Who had been talking? Who knew? Linda looked over the crowd of reporters at Sarah Cooper. Sarah had been the one who told the police about the manuscript, but she doubted Sarah or the other Wharf Rats would tell the press. Besides, they didn't know about the skull.

Croud was holding up his hands, trying to quieten down the crowd, but it was having no effect at all. As the reporters continued to bombard him with questions about the podcast and the gunshot wound in the lost skull, Linda could see Croud's control over the situation slipping. He stammered out a few non-committal responses, his frustration and anger showing on his face.

"Listen, I don't know anything about this podcast or where they're getting their information," Croud's voice rose to a near-shout, as he finally snapped. "But I can assure you that our investigation has been thorough and by the book. We will not be swayed by baseless rumors or speculation, and *we will follow procedure!*"

Mayor Godson stepped forward and placed a hand on Croud's shoulder. "I think what Staff Sergeant Croud is trying to say is that we are committed to transparency and accuracy in our handling of this case. If there are any credible leads or evidence that we have overlooked, we will certainly pursue them." He beamed at the reporters.

Croud shrugged away the mayor's hand.

The damage had been done. The reporters were buzzing with excitement, their pens scribbling furiously as they jotted down notes and crafted their headlines.

Croud hurried out of the room, his face flushed with anger and embarrassment, while Mayor Godson waved as if it were the end of a rock concert.

The only thing he didn't do, thought Linda, was take a bow.

Chapter Twenty-Three.

Sarah stood at the back of the conference room at City Hall. She offered to help a photographer with his equipment and had managed to sneak past a harried-looking woman called Karen, according to her name badge, who was checking press credentials at the door.

Sarah waited with the reporters as Staff Sergeant Croud and Mayor Godson walked in, followed by Detective Sergeant Jenkins, who, Sarah noted, had a scowl on her face, and then Constable Ray Reynolds, who looked like he was wiping crumbs from around his mouth.

Sarah watched as Staff Sergeant Croud made his announcement and felt her heart sink. It wasn't murder. Sarah knew she should be relieved that there wasn't another killer turning Sea Breeze Marina into a crime scene, but this meant that Jewell was mistaken about what she'd seen that night. Charles was probably an unfaithful husband who'd just been stringing her along, and somehow he tripped, fell in the water, and drowned. Either way, her friend was hurt. Sarah berated herself for imagining all kinds of sinister happenings. She realised that she'd hoped this was another mystery she could help solve. Although she'd nearly been killed last time she dabbled in detective work, she'd secretly been missing all the excitement. "Don't be silly," she muttered to herself.

Sarah realised she'd tuned out from the press conference, and now the mayor was speaking. She hadn't seen him much since the scandal broke about the rigged talent contest, that he'd supposedly won. She noticed his bleached blond surfer look was gone, he was sporting a bit of a paunch, and his hair, which was now brown with flecks of grey, was receding away from his forehead.

She focused on what Mayor Godson was saying. "... we urge law enforcement to keep an open mind..."

Sarah could see that Staff Sergeant Croud had an annoyed look on his face as the mayor kept speaking. Linda looked surprised as well. It was confusing. First, the police were saying it wasn't a murder, and now the mayor seemed to be urging them to keep investigating as if it was one.

Just then, she heard a beeping sound. Then another. Reporters began checking their phones. Then someone shouted out a question about a skull and gunshot wounds. Everyone started calling out questions at the same time as Staff Sergeant Croud tried to calm the room down and repeated what he said before about a lack of evidence.

Then someone shouted something about a podcast.

That must be the one that Jewell listens to, Sarah thought, as Staff Sergeant Croud and the mayor tried to regain control of the unruly journalists. Sarah watched in fascination until finally the press conference ended, and the Staff Sergeant and mayor left the room. Detective Sergeant Linda Jenkins did not leave with them but was now making a beeline for Sarah.

"What do you know about this podcast?" Linda hissed, as soon as she was in earshot. "Did one of you pass on this information?"

"One of us? What do you mean?" Sarah said indignantly, as Linda took her by the elbow and steered her out of the conference room, through the City Hall foyer, and out into the street.

"Come on, we're going to get a coffee," Linda said, "and you are going to tell me everything you know about Charles D. Harrington, his disappearance and this podcast."

Linda sounded very cross, so Sarah didn't argue.

Even Natalie must have felt Linda's annoyance because when they got to The Bean Express, she served Linda with two coffees and two muffins without saying a word. Sarah and Linda sat at a small table by the window, furthest away from the counter, where Natalie was hovering and sending them curious glances.

"Did one of you—meaning you, Jewell, or Joseph—overhear anything at the marina the other day and pass on information to this podcaster person, whoever it is?" Linda asked again, in a low but fierce voice. "I know Jewell has been listening to him."

"I've listened to an episode too," Sarah said, a bit offended, "but I can assure you, none of us would have called a podcaster with important information like that. Besides, nobody knows who he is. And we didn't know a thing about the skull."

Linda narrowed her eyes and stared at Sarah for what seemed like ages, and then finally nodded. "Alright then. I had to check."

"Is it true?" Sarah asked. "About the skull and the gunshot hole? Surely that is evidence of a murder? Why didn't you tell us?" She sounded quite annoyed.

"I can't say," Linda muttered. "I'm sorry."

Sarah sighed. "Alright then. So what now?"

"I don't know," Linda said, and she didn't. "I don't have much to go on," Linda added before she sipped her coffee. "The search of Harrington's boat didn't turn up anything. No manuscript, anyway. And it's as if he didn't exist anywhere. There's nothing online about him at all. No social media, no information about his writing, absolutely nothing."

"Jewell said he was paranoid about being hacked. He didn't even let her post a picture of him on Instagram."

"Does she know what he was working on? What the manuscript is about?"

"All he told her was it was something to do with local history."

"Shell Bay's history?"

Sarah shrugged. "That's all she told me, and I think it's all Charles told her."

Linda sighed. "If we could find the manuscript," she muttered half to herself.

"So you believe Charles was murdered, don't you?" Sarah persisted.

"It doesn't matter what I believe," Linda said. "I can't just investigate without proper authorisation." She pursed her lips. "And don't you go off investigating either. Remember what happened to you last time?"

Chapter Twenty-Four.

Linda watched Sarah through the window as she walked down the hill away from The Bean Express.

She didn't feel much like going back to the office, not while Croud was still raging about the press conference. As she finished her coffee, she noticed the bookstore next door had got a new sign. That reminded her. Alex Harding, the other liveaboard in Sea Breeze Marina, was the new owner of the bookstore. She hadn't run his name through the database yet, but why not just have a chat? She could check him out later. And maybe he knew something more about Charles Harrington. And if Charles had been researching local history, maybe he'd visited the local bookstore.

Linda left The Bean Express and stood in the street facing the store.

"Whispering Tides Bookstore," she read out loud and rolled her eyes. It sounded a bit 'woo woo' for her. She hoped it wasn't filled with new-age self-help guides and incense sticks.

Linda pushed the door, and it made a jangling sound. She heard a movement from the back of the store and muffled voices.

"Hello?" she called and stood beside the cashier's counter. Alex Harding had done a lot of work, she noticed. Linda had only visited the store once or twice since she'd lived in Shell Bay. A long time ago, she'd been an avid reader, but she always seemed too busy to settle down with a book these days. As she breathed in the familiar bookstore smell, a combination of fresh print on crisp paper from the new unread books and the mustiness from the secondhand bookshelf, full of volumes gently thumbed by countless people, Linda missed it. She missed the escape into other worlds from the reality of her complicated life.

Alex Harding had reorganised. Linda remembered piles of books scattered haphazardly on tables, shelves, and even the floor, in no particular order. But now there was a large display table at the front, with neat piles of the latest bestsellers, and beyond that, rows of shelves clearly labelled with different genres and categories. Not an incense stick in sight.

Absentmindedly, Linda brushed her hand over the glossy hardback covers on the table and waited for Alex to appear. She had definitely heard voices. A vibrating noise made her jump. She looked over to the counter and saw the glow from a mobile phone. The phone buzzed for a second longer, then stopped, and the screen darkened again.

Just then, Linda heard a door open.

"Hello?" she called again. "Mr. Harding?"

She heard footsteps, and a man emerged from behind the bookshelves.

"I'm so sorry to keep you waiting," he said. "Are you looking for something in particular?"

"I'm looking for you, actually," Linda said, "if you're Alex Harding?"

"I am," he nodded, "and you are?"

"Detective Sergeant Linda Jenkins," she said and showed him her identification.

"Oh, right, I think I saw you down at the Marina," he said, smiling. "Nice to meet you." He held out his hand for her to shake.

Alex Harding was over six feet tall, and Linda had to look up at him. He was about her age, she guessed, but was in very good shape. He was lean but not skinny and had a firm grip when she shook his hand. He was wearing a long-sleeved t-shirt, but Linda noticed he had tattoos when one of his sleeves slid upwards a fraction.

"Is this about the er... discovery?" he asked.

"Yes," Linda said. "We're talking to everyone in the Marina about it."

Alex nodded. "Not sure I can help you. I only moved there about a month ago, and it was a complete shock, to be honest. I knew there was a murder at the marina a while ago because I researched the place. I figured that lightning doesn't strike twice, but I guess I was wrong."

He gave a slight smile, but his voice was grave, not making light of the situation. He was very good-looking, Linda thought, with a jolt. Her last relationship had ended badly, and she still wasn't interested in starting a new one, not even a casual fling. And the only men she spent significant time with were Staff Sergeant Croud and Ray Reynolds.

"Detective Sergeant?"

"Oh, sorry, I was miles away for a minute," Linda said, realising she was staring at Alex Harding.

Don't be an idiot. Focus.

"Did you know Charles Harrington at all?" she asked briskly. "His boat is the Scribbler's Solace."

"I know him enough to say hi," Alex said slowly, "but I haven't seen him for a while... oh, no... is it him? I mean, was he the er..."

"Yes, he has been confirmed as the victim, I'm afraid," Linda said. "We are trying to put together a full picture of what happened to him."

"Right. Again, I can't help you. I am sorry, though. He seemed like a good guy."

"And have you noticed anything out of the ordinary at the marina? Over the last couple of weeks? Anything seem suspicious to you?"

Alex tilted his head to one side, considering the question, and then he shrugged. "Can't say I have. It's pretty quiet down there, and Fiona runs a tight ship. As it were," and he smiled, "no pun intended."

"And Charles Harrington never came in here? Bought any books?"

Alex Harding shook his head. "Not since I've owned the bookstore," he said, "and I'm afraid the last owner didn't keep good records, so I don't know."

"Okay then, Mr. Harding," Linda said brightly. "Thank you for your time."

"No problem, Detective." Alex smiled again. "And it's Alex."

"Alex, then." Linda didn't return the smile. Alex Harding seemed overly anxious to be friendly in her opinion, his smile barely leaving his face since he'd shaken her hand. "I'll let you get back to your meeting."

"Meeting?" Alex looked puzzled.

"I heard voices," Linda said. "I assumed you were in the middle of a meeting back there." She gestured towards the back of the store.

"Oh!" Alex said. "No, I was just on the phone with a publisher, that's all. Sorry if I kept you waiting," he added.

"No problem," Linda said. "Thanks again."

As she left the bookstore, she glanced over at the phone, still on the counter, and wondered why Alex Harding just lied to her.

Chapter Twenty-Five.

L inda could hear Croud's voice raised an octave or two before she'd even pushed open the entrance door to the detachment.

Wenda was sitting at the reception desk, leaning back, looking like she was listening intently to what was going on.

"He's still really mad," she stage-whispered to Linda. "He hasn't stopped since the press conference."

"Who is he shouting at now?" Linda asked. "Everyone," Wenda said. "He is sharing his tantrum equally among us. He even had a go at me. Accused me of sharing information with that podcaster." She sounded offended.

"You didn't, did you?" Linda asked.

"If I had done it, I wouldn't be an 'anonymous source'," Wenda declared. "I would want the credit. Anyway, I don't know anything. I keep my head down and do my job."

"Right," Linda muttered to herself. "Sure you do."

The door behind the reception swung open. "There you are, Jenkins," Croud snapped. "Where have you been?"

"Conducting interviews, sir," Linda said. "I thought it was important to get going, now that we have a lot of press scrutiny." She kept her face deadpan.

"Scrutiny? Is that what you call it? I call it an ambush, that's what it was. Somebody," and Croud wagged his finger at Linda, "somebody deliberately leaked misinformation to the press, and I was completely ambushed today."

"It wasn't me, sir," Linda said. "But it wasn't misinformation, was it? There was a skull..."

"But it wasn't in the forensic report, Jenkins," Croud exploded once more. "The forensic report..."

"Sir," Linda interrupted. "Why don't you call Shirley Grimm? See if you can get hold of her. Because she is not returning my calls, and that is not like her."

Linda saw Ray hovering behind Croud.

"Constable Reynolds was outside the crime scene tent on the dock, and he overheard Shirley talk about the skull, didn't you, Ray?"

"That's right, sir, I did," Ray confirmed. "Sarge looked really queasy when she came out, too."

"You've known Shirley Grimm as long as I have, sir," Linda continued. "Have you ever known her to make a mistake like this? Not without at least returning a call to explain the error? And never have I known her team to lose evidence. And, sir," Linda appealed to Croud, "have you ever known the Grim Reaper to take a vacation?"

Croud was silent.

Then he pointed at Linda. "Jenkins, you and Reynolds to my office. Right now."

Croud paced back and forth behind his desk.

"Close the door," he barked, as Linda and Ray shuffled in and stood awkwardly in the small room.

Linda closed the door. "Sit down, both of you," he said and finally sat down himself. Linda and Ray sat down too. Linda braced for another burst of fury from her boss.

Instead, he just rubbed his eyes and smoothed down his hair. Then he looked at them both and finally said, "Well? Are they right? Are we a bunch of incompetent idiots?"

"Sir," Linda leaned forward, "I don't know how those reporters or that podcaster got their information, but that's not important now. I saw the forensic evidence with my own eyes. And I know what Shirley told me. And I've been talking to Sarah Cooper and Jewell Winslow..."

"Not those people who live at the marina?" Croud interrupted. "Not again, Jenkins. They meddled..."

"I know, sir."

Linda told him about her chat with Sarah Cooper.

"The thing is, sir," Linda continued. "Charles Harrington was behaving out of character, and he was afraid of something. And Jewell Winslow says she saw strangers at the marina round about the same time we believe Harrington ended up in the water. And then there are the people..."

Croud waved his hand. "There are alternative, more logical explanations, Sergeant. Harrington could have been an adulterer who didn't have the courage to tell his mistress the truth. He could have made up all that twaddle about being in danger. And then, because he was feeling guilty or sorry for himself, he drowned his sorrows and got drowned himself."

"But what about the people on the dock?" Linda wasn't giving up.

"It was dark, Jenkins. And Ms Winslow is getting on in years."

Linda remembered something. She turned to Ray. "Did we get the CCTV footage from the marina?"

"Yes, Sarge. Chad..." Ray made a face when he said the name. "Chad left it at reception about an hour ago."

"Okay then." Linda turned back to Croud.

"Sir, if we find something on the CCTV, something that corroborates Jewell's story, then can I investigate Charles Harrington's death as a murder?"

"Jenkins, you know full well that I can sanction nothing of the sort. Only the coroner has the power to do that, and..." He stopped mid-sentence, and his head bobbed.

"And what, sir? What do you know about Shirley?" Linda demanded.

"I don't know anything, not really. But I did call the coroner's office," Croud admitted.

"Did you talk to Shirley?"

"No, I did not," Croud said and fiddled with a pen on his desk. "Shirley Grimm has retired."

"Retired?" Linda and Ray said in unison.

"Yes, retired. People do that, you know. They finish work for good and get paid a handsome pension and get to relax..." Croud's face took on a dreamy look.

"But sir, Shirley Grimm said nothing about retirement. And first, the office said she was on vacation, and now she's suddenly retired, overnight? I don't buy it."

Croud sighed heavily. "I grant you, Jenkins, it was a sudden decision. But I can't do anything about it. Shirley has gone, apparently somewhere in the Caribbean, and the acting coroner says the evidence in the Harrington case points to accidental death. So there are no extra funds for a full murder inquiry."

Linda sagged in her chair.

"But," Croud continued as he leaned forward across his desk. "I agree with you, Jenkins. Something is very off about this. So, you may go poking around a bit. Just a bit." He wagged his finger at Linda and then Ray. "And if this leaks out to the damn podcaster, then this unsanctioned investigation will be dead in the water. You hear me? Dead in the water."

Ray snorted with laughter.

Linda and Croud looked at him.

"Dead in the water. Get it? Dead in the water. It's funny because..."

"Reynolds!" Croud bellowed. "Both of you, get out of my office."

Chapter Twenty-Six.

Linda drove home. She was worried about Shirley Grimm. The Grim Reaper had been around for longer than Linda had been in the police force. Shirley was a reassuring presence at crime scenes, always calm and efficient. What had caused her to retire? Had she lost the evidence and decided she wasn't up to the job anymore? But why not call Linda back?

There were so many unanswered questions in this case. Maybe Croud was right. Maybe they should just put Harrington's death down to a tragic accident and move on.

Linda pulled into the driveway. She was ready for a large glass of wine and then bed. She'd sleep on it, and maybe in the morning, she'd just close the file.

As she stepped out of her car, Linda noticed something odd. The house was dark, no lights shining through the windows, no sign of movement inside. It was unusual for this time of evening. Where was Agnes? Another evening and her chain-smoking, gossipy landlady was nowhere to be seen.

Linda approached the house, a sense of unease growing in the pit of her stomach. She knocked on the door; the sound echoing through the stillness. No answer. She tried the handle, surprised to find it unlocked. Agnes was many things, but careless about security wasn't one of them.

Pushing the door open, Linda stepped inside, the musty smell of stale cigarette smoke and mothballs hitting her like a wave. The house was old and shabby, the walls stained a sickly yellow from years of nicotine exposure. "Agnes?" Linda called out, her voice sounding too loud in the eerie quiet. "Are you home?"

No response. Linda reached for the light switch, flicking it on. The dim, flickering bulb cast a sickly glow over the living room, revealing a scene of utter chaos.

The room had been ransacked. Cushions were torn from the sofa, their stuffing spilling out like entrails. Drawers had been yanked from the cabinets, their contents strewn across the floor. The old television lay on its side, the screen shattered. And everywhere, the scattered remains of Agnes' knick-knacks, the porcelain figurines, and glass trinkets lay in shattered pieces on the stained carpet.

"Agnes!" Linda called out, her heart thumping.

She moved further into the house, her hand instinctively reaching for the latex gloves she always carried in her purse. The kitchen was in a similar state of disarray, dishes smashed on the floor, the contents of the refrigerator spilled across the linoleum.

Linda stood still and listened. As much as she wanted to run from room to room looking for Agnes, it was possible whoever had done this might still be in the house.

Linda heard nothing. It was silent, no creaks or sounds of breathing even.

Then Linda moved. She took the stairs up to the second floor, two at a time. Linda had never been up here before and had no idea how many rooms there were.

When she got to the landing, she saw that every door was open.

Cautiously, she moved from room to room, calling out at every doorway. "Agnes, are you there? Police."

Each room was the same. Cupboard doors were open, linen and towels were on the floors, the contents of every drawer dumped out.

In the largest bedroom, which Linda assumed was where Agnes slept, the mattress had been flipped, the sheets torn and scattered. But there was no sign of Agnes.

Linda jogged downstairs again.

She reached in her back pocket for her phone, her fingers trembling as she tapped in the number for the detachment. She'd worked many break-ins during her career, but this was different. She was surprised at the anxiety she was feeling about Agnes' whereabouts. She'd become attached to the old bat, she thought as she waited for the call to connect.

"Barrie? It's Linda." Linda reported the break-in to the duty constable, who promised to dispatch a cruiser.

"Thanks," Linda said and ended the call. She should leave the house, she thought. She didn't want to contaminate the crime scene. Linda took one more look in the kitchen. She remembered that Agnes had a walk-in pantry, big enough for someone to hide in.

But the pantry door was open, and tins of food were knocked all over the floor. It had been a thorough job, Linda thought. She was about to leave when she saw Agnes' purse lying on the kitchen counter.

It was unzipped. With one gloved finger, Linda opened it and peered in. Cash was in there.

She went back into the living room.

Nothing valuable had been taken. This wasn't a robbery, Linda thought. Whoever did this was looking for something specific. And where the hell was Agnes? Had she run off in fright?

Then a thought occurred to Linda. What about her place? She backed out of the living room, but as she did, she caught sight of a stain on the carpet, which made her stomach flip.

It was dark and congealing, but it was definitely blood.

Linda heard police sirens getting louder.

She left the house and ran to her front door. Everything looked normal, except for an envelope left there on the doorstep. It was a courier's delivery and addressed to her. Linda shoved it in her purse for later.

She fumbled for her key and put it in the lock, but the door swung inward.

"Oh no," she breathed as she turned on the light in the hallway. Her apartment had been trashed too.

Chapter Twenty-Seven.

"You're kidding, Sarge." Ray Reynolds's eyes were wide. "Why would anyone break into Agnes Crofton's house? To steal her ashtrays?"

"Of course I'm not kidding," Linda snapped. She was tired. She'd been up all night, watching the crime scene techs process the chaotic scene at Agnes' house and then her apartment. Then it had taken her two hours to clean up before she fell into bed in the early hours, just after she'd interrogated a technician for preliminary information.

"The good news is that there is very little blood," the technician had told her. "So the lady wasn't bludgeoned to death. Or stabbed," he said helpfully, but then paused. "But she could have been strangled, I suppose. That doesn't cause any blood."

Linda had resisted the urge to slap him.

"If killing Agnes was the point of this," she said. "Then why didn't he—or they—leave the body here? Why move her?"

"That's a great point," the technician agreed. "I have no idea. That's why you're the detective, I suppose." He'd waved an evidence bag at her just before he left. "Partial prints on the front door." He beamed cheerfully.

Ray got Linda a cup of coffee.

"Thank you," she said. "I have no concrete evidence for this, Ray, but I think this is connected to the Harrington case. I don't think Agnes knew Harrington. She certainly never went near the marina. She never went out at all, as far as I know. But I feel it in my gut..."

Linda's voice trailed off. "What is it, Sarge?"

"The podcast," Linda said wearily. "The stupid podcast. Agnes was listening to it."

"Everyone in town is listening to it, Sarge," Ray pointed out.

"Yes, you're right. It's just... I don't know," Linda shook her head, "it wasn't a robbery, Ray. Her TV was still there, and her purse with all the cash in it. And nothing was taken from my apartment. It was as if someone was looking for something. And why would they want Agnes? Where have they taken her?"

Ray wrinkled his nose. "Can't imagine," he said. "But a few hours of her and they'll soon change their mind."

Linda gave herself a shake. "New investigation, Constable. But we won't rule out a connection to the Harrington case. While we wait for forensics, I want you to check her phone records. See what comes up."

Ray nodded. "Do you have her number?"

Linda reached into her purse for a pen to write it down for Ray. Her fingers brushed something, and she pulled out the envelope that had been delivered the night before.

"What's that?" Ray asked.

"No idea," Linda said. "It was by my door last night, special delivery." She turned it over. "No return address."

Linda tore the envelope open. Inside was a folded piece of paper. She pulled it out, and lay it on the desk.

It was a photograph—poor quality and grainy because it was printed on ordinary paper.

"Ray," Linda pushed it over to him, "look at this."

Ray peered at it. "But that looks like..." He looked at her. "Is it what I think it is?"

Linda nodded. "Yes, Ray. That's exactly what it is."

Chapter Twenty-Eight.

Mayor Gordon Godson was feeling pleased with himself. An hour earlier, he called out to Karen, his assistant, that he was going to be busy doing some very important work and should not be disturbed.

She'd stopped typing at her keyboard and swiveled around on her chair. "What important work?" she asked in a tone of voice that suggested she didn't believe him at all.

"It's confidential," he told her.

"Sure. Confidential," she repeated slowly before she turned back to her computer screen, but not quickly enough to hide her eye roll.

Gordon made a mental note—and then a written one, because he could never remember the mental notes he made—to remind Karen of the Staff Code of Conduct rulebook, in which Gordon was sure there were regulations that outlawed eye rolling, sniggering, and sarcasm. And if there were not, he made another note to bring it up at the next council meeting and make a motion. Or a resolution. He always got those two mixed up.

Gordon settled himself down in his leather chair, kicked his shoes off, put his feet up on the desk, and popped his earplugs in. Then he selected the latest podcast episode from the Shadowcaster, entitled 'Death on the Dock' and pressed play.

After listening carefully for an hour, he allowed himself a victory air punch. Not only was there no mention of the Neon Dreamers or the cloud hanging over his singing career, but the Shadowcaster had actually said that he was the hero of the hour.

"It's clear from the latest press conference, led by Staff Sergeant Croud of Shell Bay RCMP, that a disgraceful police cover-up is occurring right now in this small town where tensions are running high after the discovery of a corpse at Sea Breeze Marina. Mayor Godson, showing honour and courage in the face of this deep state conspiracy, urged the residents of Shell Bay to remain vigilant until the murderer had been apprehended. He begged Staff Sergeant Croud to do his duty and protect Shell Bay citizens and not cower before those who would cover up the truth, and then, in an unprecedented turn of events, ordered Staff Sergeant Croud to continue investigating this incident as a full-blown homicide. The people of Shell Bay are counting on you, Mayor Godson said, and so am I. He was truly the hero of the hour."

Gordon swiped the screen of his phone, closed his eyes, and listened to that bit again.

"Excuse me, Mayor Godson." A voice came from far away. Then there was a firm rap on Gordon's desk. He jerked out of his seat and nearly toppled to the floor.

"What the heck?" Gordon exclaimed, pulling the plugs out of his ears and glaring at the man who had interrupted him.

The man waited while Gordon straightened his shirt and slipped his feet back under the desk, feeling around for his shoes.

"Who let you in?" Gordon demanded, giving up on his shoes.

The man gestured towards the door. "A lady outside. She said to come right in, you weren't busy at all. My apologies if I startled you."

"You didn't. And I was. Busy, I mean. I was, er... listening to something important. Anyway, who are you? And what do you want? Er, I mean, how can I help you?" Gordon adjusted his tone. "Are you a journalist?" Gordon asked, trying to sound casual and not suspicious.

"Were you listening to the Shadowcaster?" the man asked, ignoring Gordon's question.

"No. I mean, maybe. Yes, yes, I was. Why?" Gordon stuttered.

The man raised his hand and smiled. "Of course you were. Everyone is listening to the Shadowcaster at the moment."

Gordon half-smiled back. The man was very average-looking. Brown hair, neither dark brown nor light brown, not long, but not overly short. He had blue eyes? Or grey? And he was dressed in a blue jacket and grey pants. There was nothing out of the ordinary about this man, but Gordon suddenly felt uneasy.

"Who did you say you are?" Gordon asked again.

"I didn't. I work for some very influential people who have been watching you," the man said. "May I sit down?" His tone was friendly enough, but Gordon sensed an underlying authority, as if this man was used to getting his own way.

He didn't wait for Gordon to answer. Instead, he pulled a chair up to the desk and sat facing Gordon.

"Watching me? Why? What did I do?" Gordon felt a hot flush start at the base of his neck and then spread upwards to his face.

"Don't worry, Gordon. They like what they see. And they'd like to offer you... some assistance."

"An assistant? I already have an assistant," Gordon said while wondering if there was some way he could fire Karen for letting this man into his office.

"Not an assistant. *Assistance*. In the form of money," the man said patiently. "Lots and lots of money."

"Oh, that sounds like a bribe," Gordon said. "I can't take money from a stranger. Anyway, I have lots of money. I was once..."

"A rockstar?" the man inquired, smiling slightly. Then, he leaned forward and said in a low voice which made the back of Gordon's neck tingle, "Mayor, what we are proposing is the death of Gordon Godson, the lead singer of the Neon Dreamers..."

"What?" Gordon gasped, leaning back as far away as he could.

"And the birth of Mayor Gordon Godson, the most celebrated and loved elected official in the history of Shell Bay. Or Vancouver Island. Or the..."

"Oh, that's a relief. For a minute, I thought you were going to kill me." Gordon gave a nervous laugh.

The man just nodded.

"So... er, how do you intend to make me... um... loved and celebrated then?" Gordon asked, still nervous but intrigued now.

"As I was saying, we have lots of money. And we'd like to give it to you to spend on the town."

"Oh, you mean a grant?" Gordon was relieved. "Did we fill in some kind of application?"

"Not exactly." The man's expression did not change, but his voice had an impatient edge to it. "We propose to give you a million dollars."

"A million dollars?" Gordon was stunned. "But that's... that's very generous of you..."

"Yes, yes, it is. We only have one criterion that you must agree to. Before we transfer the funds," the man said. "Well, two actually."

"And what are they?" Gordon's eyes widened as the man leaned forward again and beckoned Gordon to come nearer with his finger.

"Listen very carefully..."

Chapter Twenty-Nine.

Linda tried to organise her thoughts, which were lurching off in all directions.

"So this confirms it, Sarge," Ray said, tapping the piece of paper on the murder board. The image, although grainy, clearly showed a human skull with tufts of hair, turned to one side to reveal a perfectly round hole.

"This is the skull you saw, right? But where did the photograph come from? The Grim Reaper?"

"It must be from her. Who else? But why not call and explain? It makes no sense. I need more coffee."

Linda tried to clear the fog from her brain with more caffeine.

Ray pinned the photograph on the board and stood back.

"What's this?" Croud came into the conference room. He saw Linda sipping from her coffee cup. "Jenkins, you look terrible. What happened?"

Linda explained about the break-ins.

"Good God. But they didn't take anything?" Croud asked, sounding shocked.

"Just Agnes," Ray commented.

"No, sir," Linda added, giving Ray a withering look. "They were obviously looking for something."

"What?"

"Maybe the manuscript?" Ray suggested helpfully.

Croud looked at him, confused. "What are you talking about? What manuscript?"

Linda groaned inwardly. "I told you about the manuscript, sir."

"No, Detective Sergeant, you didn't. So start talking and tell me about that photograph too," Croud snapped, pointing at the murder board.

It took twenty minutes for Linda to tell Croud about the manuscript. Again.

"Why didn't you tell me before?" he demanded.

" I did, sir. But, sir, we've never seen the thing," Linda explained wearily. "Not even Jewell has seen it. We don't know if it exists. At the moment, we have virtually no evidence of a murder—except for that picture."

Croud examined the grainy image. "And you received this in the mail?"

"Yes, sir. No return address and no note."

He sighed. "It's not admissible in court," he said, "and someone might have used EI and Photostore to make it."

"You mean AI and Photoshop, sir?"

"Whatever. But there are too many strange things happening around here, Jenkins. Your theory is that Harrington is somehow connected with Agnes Crofton?"

"It's just a theory, sir," Linda admitted. "We haven't made a solid connection yet."

"You had better get on with it," Croud said. "It's possible that forensics from Agnes Crofton's house will help us with the Harrington murder."

"Murder? Did you say murder, sir?"

"Yes, I did, Jenkins. And I want it solved."

Chapter Thirty.

"Agnes Crofton? No, he never mentioned her," Jewell said, creasing her brow as she dug back into her memory. "I told you, he didn't talk about his work at all. All I know is that it had something to do with local history. I got the impression that Charles had family who lived in Shell Bay a long time ago. But nothing stands out. Sorry."

"That's okay," Linda said. Her head was thumping, and she would have loved to go home and sleep for a few hours. But she couldn't waste a minute. Agnes' life might be in danger. So she'd made her way down to the marina to talk to Jewell again.

"Agnes would have been someone to talk to about local history, though," Linda said, rubbing her eyes and stifling a yawn. "She knows everyone and everything that goes on in this town."

"I hope she's alright," Jewell said anxiously. "I wish I could help more. But Charles didn't even talk about his research. He didn't visit the museum or anything, as far as I know."

"He couldn't have visited Shell Bay Museum," Linda smiled, patting Jewell's hand. "It's closed down. Never mind. If you think of anything at all..."

Linda's cell phone buzzed. She glanced at the screen and sighed. "Sir? What's happened?"

Chapter Thirty-One.

"In a world where darkness reigns, one voice emerges from the shadows to uncover the truth. Welcome to Shadowcaster's Sinister Symposium, your source for the most captivating true crime stories. Tonight, we'll peel back more layers of a perplexing mystery that has left even the most seasoned detectives scratching their heads. This is Episode Three of a mystery which I am calling Death on the Dock."

"Do people listen to this nonsense?" Croud blurted, his head bobbing furiously.

Linda was sitting in his office with her cell phone on the desk.

Mayor Godson had called Croud when Linda was at the marina with Jewell.

"He says we need to have another press conference right away," Croud bellowed at Linda. "He says we have to shut down all the investigations because we look like bloody idiots, and I'm inclined to agree with him. Get back here, now Jenkins."

Croud had picked up his rant as soon as Linda walked back into the office.

"I told you to poke around discreetly, Jenkins, and what happens? Details of our investigation get broadcast to everyone and his dog in Shell Bay."

"Where's Ray?" Linda asked, ignoring Croud.

"Gone home," chirped Wenda.

Linda shepherded Croud into his office and closed the door. "Sir," she said, "let's listen to the podcast first, shall we? Maybe this idiot is just speculating and got lucky. When we know what we're dealing with, you can just issue a statement and deny everything."

Croud had calmed down. Linda googled "Shadowcaster," and the podcast popped up.

It wasn't an amateur production, Linda had to admit, even though the introduction was sensationalist and frankly a little cheesy. But as the episode continued, it was obvious that the Shadowcaster's information was worryingly accurate and detailed.

Not only that, he painted a less than complimentary picture of the Shell Bay police investigation so far.

"Is this incompetence? Lack of training? Or worse than that, a wilful cover-up of a gruesome murder? And why was Charles D. Harrington killed? To some, he was a respected writer, living out his retirement in the tranquil surroundings of Sea Breeze Marina, but to others, he was the keeper of sinister secrets, which, if revealed, would lead to the exposure of scandalous truths. What do the police know about Harrington's manuscript, and why are they hiding its existence from the public?"

"I only found out about the damn manuscript today," grumbled Croud. "How can I be hiding it from the public if I didn't know about it?"

"Shh," Linda said. "Sir."

"And now another poor soul has been injured, possibly due to the bungling Shell Bay police department. Poor Agnes Crofton, a sweet old lady, was abducted, her home ransacked. Is she another victim of the killer? How many more victims before the police do their job?"

"He doesn't know that much, sir," Linda said. "He called Agnes a sweet old lady. I think he's got wind of a few details, and he's stringing it into a story."

"Hmm." Croud's face had returned to its normal colour.

"And he knows about the possible existence of a manuscript, but he doesn't know much about it. He mentioned scandalous truths. That is a bit vague."

"Jenkins." Croud sat up suddenly. "Could the shadow-thingy pod man be our killer?"

Linda thought. "It's possible, sir. But why keep drawing attention to himself by broadcasting? And if the killer is looking for the manuscript because they don't want it made public, then why keep mentioning it?"

"To flush out where it is?" Croud suggested. "Get some idiot to phone in with the whereabouts?"

Linda hadn't thought of that, she was about to admit when her phone vibrated.

"Ray?" she said when she answered, expecting to hear from her constable.

"Not Ray," said an irritated female voice. "It's Natalie."

"Natalie?" Linda couldn't place the name.

"From The Bean Express."

"Erm, well, I don't know if we want to order muffins right now," Linda said. "I'm a bit busy."

"I hope you are," Natalie replied at the other end of the line in a sarcastic tone. "You need to be looking for my Auntie Agnes."

Chapter Thirty-Two.

Linda heard the crunch of wheels on the gravel driveway. She opened the front door and looked out to see Natalie getting out of a smart pickup truck. The girl looked smaller than she did in the cafe, and as she walked over to Linda, she seemed deflated. Her shoulders were hunched and she was struggling to carry a cardboard box.

Linda walked out to meet her. "Let me help you with that," she said.

"I can manage," Natalie snapped, her usual spark of attitude returning. Now that Linda knew Natalie was Agnes' niece, she could see the resemblance.

It had taken a few minutes for Natalie to persuade Linda that she really was related to Agnes Crofton. Yes, Agnes had a sister (estranged from Agnes), and Natalie was the sister's daughter, therefore Agnes' niece.

"This is not hard. If you can't figure this out, then my aunt is doomed," Natalie had said during their phone call. Linda could picture the girl rolling her eyes.

Natalie had insisted that she had information that would help Linda find her aunt.

"It's private," she'd told Linda. "I'm not coming into the detachment."

So Linda had invited Natalie to her apartment.

"Come in, then," Linda said and held out the door for Natalie. "Just put the box on the kitchen table."

Natalie did so and then looked around. "Still the same dump," she remarked. "You know my grandmother died in here, right?"

Linda nodded. "I do."

She offered Natalie a seat. "You want a coffee or something?" Linda asked.

"Do you have wine?"

Linda narrowed her eyes and debated asking Natalie how old she was, then decided against it. In the cafe, Natalie had the air of someone older than she did now. Sitting in Linda's kitchen, she looked like a child.

Linda got two glasses out of the kitchen cupboard and then bent down to find the emergency bottle of red she kept under the sink.

"Do you hide your wine from Aunt Agnes?" Natalie asked, sounding amused.

"I have to," Linda said, straightening up. "She snoops in here all the time. She doesn't even try to hide it."

"Sounds like Auntie," Natalie said. "She's always looking for information." Her face darkened. "That's probably what got her..."

"There's no evidence that she is dead," Linda cut in, "if that's what you're thinking."

"Is there any evidence that she is still alive?" Natalie shot back.

"There is evidence of a break-in," Linda answered calmly, "and evidence to suggest that whoever broke in was looking for something. But if somebody wanted to kill Agnes, then why wouldn't they have just done that and left her body? If they went to the trouble of taking her, then my guess is that your aunt is alive. And today, if you can tell me everything you know, we might be able to figure out why."

Linda opened the bottle of wine and poured two glasses. "Are you ready?" she asked.

"These are some of my aunt's private documents," Natalie started, pointing at the box. "You can have them. Agnes gave me instructions to give them to you if anything ever happened to her."

"To me? Why?" Linda was startled.

"Because she trusted you. She liked you too. Anyway, she told me what I am about to tell you. Those were her instructions. Give you the box and tell you the stuff. And drink your wine." Natalie smirked. "I made the last bit up."

"Hilarious. Continue, please..." Linda waved her hand. She was secretly pleased that Agnes liked her.

"A long time ago in Shell Bay," Natalie started, "my grandmother Eliza was the curator of Shell Bay Museum, and my grandfather was the Staff Sergeant at Shell Bay detachment."

"Really? That's fascinating. I mean, that old museum is derelict now..."

Natalie fixed Linda with a stare. "Let me finish," she said. "It will take all night if you keep interrupting. Just be quiet and keep topping up my wine."

Linda nodded.

"Anyway, my grandmother was the 'keeper of knowledge' for the town, sort of. She knew things, kept secrets, and collected information. Documents and stuff. And things for the museum. She helped my grandfather because he was the only police officer in town. Many people were arrested and charged because of stuff my grandmother knew."

"I bet she was popular," muttered Linda sarcastically.

"Shell Bay was not like it is now," Natalie continued. "There was lots of crime. Smuggling and corruption, that sort of thing. The mayor was far worse than the one we have now. My grandfather was busy. But one night, he witnessed a murder." Natalie paused dramatically and took a sip of wine.

"Someone quite influential got drunk and killed someone," she said. "Right in front of my grandfather. Well, he immediately arrested this person and put him in jail. They tried to bribe him, but Henry, my grandfather, did not take the money. He said he was going to charge this person with murder, and that was that."

"Who was this person?" Linda asked.

"I don't know," Natalie said. "Nobody knows. On the way home from the police station after putting the murderer in a holding cell, my grandfather was murdered."

"Oh, my goodness."

"Yes. We don't know who did it. We assume that a friend of the influential person killed my grandfather and then set the murderer free, and removed all the evidence from the police station. They were trying to cover up the whole incident. But what they didn't know was that my grandmother had been in the police station that night and had overheard all the evidence against this influential person. The next morning, when my grandfather hadn't returned home, my grandmother went back there and found the holding cell empty and the office ransacked. Then, she found my grandfather. She was the only person alive who knew about the arrest."

"So she was able to give evidence? He was still charged?"

Natalie looked at Linda as if she were an idiot.

"No, of course not. She didn't want to get killed too. She kept her secret for years. Both murders went unsolved. And this influential person went on to be more powerful and have a family. And that family is still very powerful today."

She took another slurp of wine.

Linda was confused. 'How do you know?" she asked, "About the influential person—the murderer—becoming powerful?"

"It was years later that my grandmother told my mother and my Aunt Agnes who exactly my grandfather had arrested and what happened that night. My mother thought it was all nonsense because my grandmother was old and made a lot of stuff up, but Agnes believed her. Not only that, Agnes tried to dig up more information about the people who were behind my grandfather's murder."

"I see," Linda said slowly, seeing where this story was going.

"As you know, my aunt has a talent for getting information," Natalie continued. "She found that the influential person and his powerful family had formed an organisation which likes to... influence people. To get what they want."

"And then what?" Linda was still trying to get this all straight in her mind.

"By this time, my grandmother was ill, and she lived... here." Natalie waved her hand around. "One day, Aunt Agnes came home and found my grandmother dead. But she hadn't died of natural causes, according to the coroner. She had been strangled. Well, Aunt Agnes was convinced her mother had been murdered by people working for this organisation, and she kicked up a stink. But they were powerful enough to cover it all up. The coroner changed the report, but there was a nasty rumour which went around that Aunt Agnes had killed her. It was horrible."

"I have to ask two questions," Linda interrupted. "First, did Agnes tell you who the murderer was? And what was the name of the organisation?"

"Is," Natalie corrected. "The name IS the Nautilus Circle. And Auntie has never told me the name of the murderer."

"Who was the coroner?"

"That's three questions." Natalie held out her glass for a top up of wine.

Linda glared at Natalie and didn't make a move to fill it.

"Shirley Grimm," Natalie said. "It was her first case."

Linda closed her eyes. It was starting to make sense. "So, you think this Nautilus Circle is still operating?"

"Of course it is," Natalie snapped. "Who do you think kidnapped my aunt?"

"But why didn't they just kill her?" Linda wondered out loud.

"Because they want the manuscript," Natalie said, as if it was obvious. "It's all about the Nautilus Circle and their crimes."

"But Harrington wrote the manuscript," Linda questioned, getting confused. "How did Agnes get it?"

"Harrington wrote the manuscript with Agnes' help," Natalie said, exasperated.

"But why was Harrington writing about the Nautilus Circle in the first place?" Linda still didn't get it.

Natalie reached over to the box of documents she'd brought with her. She handed Linda a black and white photograph.

It was a picture of a severe-looking woman, with a striking resemblance to Agnes, standing beside a man in a police uniform, and a younger man standing beside them both. Linda recognised the museum building in the background, looking in much better shape than it did now.

"You remember the murder my grandfather witnessed? The one that got him killed? The victim worked for my grandmother at the museum. His name was Douglas Harrington. Charles Douglas Harrington's father."

Chapter Thirty-Three.

The sun had just begun to set, casting a warm golden glow over Shell Bay Marina.

Jewell sat alone on her deck, clutching a glass of wine in one hand and her phone in the other. A shawl was draped around her shoulders, and a book lay on the arm of the chair. Usually, Jewell loved September evenings. The marina was quiet, the summer visitors long gone, and the only sounds were the gentle rocking of the boats as they bumped against the docks and the occasional splash of a curious seal or otter playing in the receding tide.

On other evenings, when Jewell wasn't worried or stressed, she would sit outside, huddled under a blanket until the sky darkened and transformed into a canvas of stars, the ocean a wide expanse of inky black. She felt happy to be alive and content with her life on The Little Gem.

But tonight was different. Jewell wasn't looking at the ocean; her mind was far away, and her heart heavy.

Charles was gone, and with him, Jewell supposed, her chance of having a special someone in her life. Yes, Charles had been a bit pompous and had an irritating way of 'mansplaining', as Sarah called it, but he seemed genuinely interested in Jewell's life. He'd appreciated her artsy, bohemian style and had solemnly declared her 'a rising talent in the renaissance of the arts and crafts movement'.

She wished she hadn't been so quick to suspect he'd lied to her. She was certain now that the woman she'd heard on his boat that night had something to do with his death. She must have been looking for whatever Charles had been working on. His writing was the only thing he hadn't discussed with Jewell.

"Best not talk about that, ol' gal," he'd said to her, tapping his nose and winking when she'd asked about the book he was writing. Jewell had thought that maybe Charles was one of those writers who didn't like to talk about their work until it was finished, so she hadn't pressed him further.

Her phone vibrated in her hand, pulling her out of her thoughts. She tapped the green icon and accepted the call.

"Jewell? Are you sitting on your deck?" Sarah's voice said.

"Yes," Jewell sighed.

"Do you have wine?"

"Yes," Jewell said again.

"Good. Then I'm coming over. I have an idea." The phone went dead.

Jewell sighed again, then stood up and stretched. She went into her cabin to get another glass and the half-full bottle of red wine.

As she came out of the cabin, she felt the boat rock gently as Sarah stepped onto the deck.

Sarah held up another bottle of wine. "I thought we might need more than one glass," she explained.

"Was your idea to get completely wasted?" Jewell asked. "Because that sounds okay to me."

"No," Sarah said. "I've been thinking about Charles' manuscript. I think that's what got him..." She stopped suddenly and looked at Jewell.

"Killed?" Jewell said, her voice trembling slightly. "That's what you were going to say, wasn't it?"

Sarah nodded. "I'm so sorry, Jewell," she said, her face sad.

"Here," Jewell said, wiping a stray tear from her cheek and putting down the wine and glass on the table. "Pull up a chair. I'll get you a blanket, and then you can tell me about your idea. Anything is better than sitting here in self-pity."

When the two women were settled in their chairs, holding a glass of wine each, Jewell asked, "So, what were you thinking about Charles' manuscript?"

"We know it's not on Charles' boat," Sarah confirmed.

Jewell nodded. "Maybe that woman found it and took it," she said. "After she and whoever she was with killed him and dumped him in the ocean." She sighed. "I'm just trying to accept that he's gone and never coming back." She looked at Sarah, her voice breaking. "It's so hard."

"I know," Sarah said, reaching over to grab Jewell's hand. "I know it must be so hard to make sense of all this. That's why I can't stop thinking about his writing. What was he working on that was so important that someone would want to kill him?"

"Well, it's long gone," Jewell said resignedly. "We'll never know now."

"I don't think so," Sarah said firmly.

"The point is that someone killed Charles, and his manuscript is missing. And now, Agnes Crofton is missing, and her house is trashed. I think the person—or persons—who were looking for Charles' work didn't find it and went looking at Agnes Crofton's place."

"But why would Agnes Crofton have it?" Jewell said. "As far as I know, Charles didn't know her. He never said, anyway."

"No idea," Sarah said, "but that isn't the point either."

"So, what is the damn point?" Jewell was getting more confused, and a little irritated. "I wish you'd get to it."

"My point is," Sarah said, sounding excited, "I think they—whoever they are—haven't found the manuscript. And what's more, I think I know where it is."

Jewell snorted. "Have you been vaping with Chad? Are you high?"

"Of course not. And," Sarah continued in an offended tone, "don't you want to know where I think it is?"

"Where?" Jewell rolled her eyes, although it was a lot darker now, and she was sure Sarah couldn't see.

"Here," Sarah announced triumphantly.

"Where?" Jewell squinted in the twilight to see if Sarah was holding it. "You've got it?"

"No, silly, you have it."

"What are you talking about? If I had it, I would have given it to the police. Are you sure you haven't been vaping?"

"No, no, you don't understand. You have it, but you don't know you have it."

"I do? I don't?" None of this was making sense to Jewell, and she was getting tired.

"Yes, you do. Have the manuscript, I mean. I think Charles left it here, on your boat. I think he hid it on your boat. You said he was behaving strangely before he disappeared, didn't you? Was he ever on your boat alone?"

Jewell hesitated. "You know, I did find him on my boat one afternoon. He was just coming out of the engine room. He'd said he had been—"

"But what if he was hiding the manuscript?" Sarah replied, and even in the darkness, Jewell could see Sarah's eyes shining with excitement. "What if he knew that someone was after it, and he put it somewhere they wouldn't think to look?"

Jewell was silent once more. Then, "You're right," Jewell put her wine-glass down. "Well, what are we waiting for? Let's look."

Sarah stood up. "I was hoping you'd say that," she said, then stopped. "Did you hear that?"

"What?" Jewell stood up too. "I can't hear anything."

"I'm sure I heard something. It was kind of a shuffling sound," Sarah said. Both women stood still and quiet on the deck of The Little Gem and listened, but all they heard was the soft lapping of the waves and the occasional creak of the wooden docks.

"Must have been an otter," Sarah said, "pooping on the dock, I bet. Come on, Jewell, let's start looking."

Jewell stood in the middle of the cabin, her sharp eyes scanning the bookcases, then the storage cupboards. "I suppose we just start in the obvious places," she said doubtfully. "There aren't many places to hide anything on the boat, you know that."

"I'll start in the cupboards," Sarah said. "Why don't you search your stateroom? Under the bunk, that sort of thing."

"Alright, let's do this," Jewell muttered under her breath as she stepped into her stateroom and looked around. Like the galley, there wasn't much storage space. Liveaboards learned two things when they first abandoned living permanently on solid ground: first, possessions became far less important, and second, neatness was everything.

It didn't take long for Jewell to check every nook and cranny, even under the mattress. Nothing.

"Anything?" Sarah called from the galley.

"No, not a thing. You?"

Jewell stepped out of the stateroom and into the small galley. Sarah was crouched down, peering under the sink. "Nothing yet. Did you check your bathroom?"

Jewell opened the narrow bathroom door. The space was tiny, and the cupboard over the sink only had enough room for Jewell's toothpaste and bottle of shampoo.

"Sarah, I don't think Charles hid anything here," she said as she came out of the bathroom. "I think it's more likely that the people who killed Charles found the manuscript on his boat. The other break-in is just a coincidence."

Jewell suddenly felt very tired and sat down heavily on her armchair.

Sarah closed the door under the sink and came to sit beside Jewell, taking a seat at the galley table.

"Jewell, I don't believe in coincidences," she said firmly. "And even that podcaster, you know, the one you're always listening to—he said there was something strange going on."

"You've listened to the Shadowcaster?" Jewell was surprised. "I thought..."

"I know," Sarah said, "but everyone was listening, and well, I thought I'd check out what the fuss was about. But I only listened to the last episode, and it was all about the body... sorry, the victim, Charles." Sarah changed her words as Jewell's face crumpled and tears fell.

"Sorry," Jewell wiped her cheek with the back of her hand. "It's just thinking about Charles as a body and not a person anymore."

Sarah reached over and put her hand on Jewell's arm, squeezing it.

Jewell composed herself. "What did the Shadowcaster say?"

"Not much that helps," Sarah admitted, "but he did say that the police were trying to cover up a murder. He said that his sources informed him that the forensics had found evidence the victim had been shot, but the police denied it."

"What about my statement?" Jewell asked. "About what happened that night?"

"The police haven't said anything about that," Sarah said. She got up from her seat at the galley table and moved around so she was facing Jewell. She knelt in front of Jewell and grabbed both hands in hers.

"Jewell," she said firmly, "the only people who believe that Charles was murdered are you, me, and Shadowcaster. The only way we can prove it and force the police to get justice for Charles is to find that manuscript and find out what he was working on that got him killed. Is there anywhere else you can think of that Charles might have stashed it? Think, Jewell," she coaxed.

Jewell closed her eyes and thought back to the times that Charles had spent on The Little Gem. He'd regularly shared a bottle of wine with her on the deck on warm evenings over the last couple of months. She'd cooked dinner for him, and they'd eaten in the snug cabin at the galley table. And then Charles relaxed with a brandy in this very chair.

"The thing is, Sarah," Jewell said at last, "Charles never brought anything onto the boat except a bottle of wine. He never had a briefcase or..." Then she stopped, remembering something.

"What is it?" Sarah gripped Jewell's arm again. "You've remembered something?"

"I'm an idiot. He checked my bilge pump," Jewell cried. "He told me. He said he'd been in the engine room and now it was working perfectly."

"How do we get into the engine room?" Sarah asked urgently. "We have to check it."

"The hatch is on the deck," Jewell said, and both women hurried out of the cabin. It was pitch-black outside, and it took a few moments for their eyes to adjust.

"Should I get a flashlight?" Jewell asked, as Sarah found the hatch and began pulling the cover off.

"Yes, I can't see a thing."

In minutes, Jewell was handing Sarah the flashlight, and she was climbing down into the engine room.

"Ooh, there's not much room in here," Sarah's voice echoed. "Where's the bilge?"

"The bow," Jewell called, then remembering that Sarah was still a boating novice added, "the pointy end."

There were a few more minutes of grunts from Sarah and then a "Damn it," followed by... "Jewell, I've found it!"

"You have? You're sure it's the manuscript?" Jewell called out.

Sarah emerged from the hatch carrying a large plastic bag, looking triumphant. "Here it is, Jewell. Now we're getting somewhere!"

Chapter Thirty-Four

Chad Garner heard the excited voices from The Little Gem and nearly wet himself with relief. He finally had some information, and now, maybe, this whole ordeal would be over.

He was going straight from now on, he promised himself. He would never, ever break the law again. He wouldn't even steal a bicycle.

He realised his hands were shaking. Ever since he'd hit that elderly woman over the head in her kitchen the other night, he had barely been able to function. What if he killed her? And his fingerprints must be everywhere. He'd put gloves on at the last minute, but he was sure he'd touched the front door. And the Detective Sergeant lived right next door. He'd trashed that place too, so now he'd be on the hook for smashing up a copper's home. He was right in the muck, up to his neck.

If he got caught, then everyone would think it was revenge for his brother. Nobody would believe that he was being *forced* to break the law.

If he got away with this, then it was the straight and narrow path for him.

Chad crept down the dock to the boathouse. This was where he was supposed to make his report. He stood and shivered in the darkness.

He was being set up. Chad was smart enough to figure that out. He was a patsy. He'd doctored the CCTV footage as he'd been ordered to. He'd trashed two houses and had taken out that old woman, and he'd hung around the dock every night spying on the liveaboards.

There was no trace of the mysterious man who was threatening Chad's life. All the evidence would point to Chad, and all he had was a story about a man he'd never seen.

He was totally screwed, he thought miserably.

"Well?" A hand clamped on Chad's shoulder from behind. "Don't move. What did you hear?"

Chad told him.

He heard a grunt of approval in the darkness, and the hand loosened its grip. "Tomorrow," the voice growled, "you have work to do. Be here at the same time."

Just as the figure retreated into the shadows of the boathouse, Chad moved his head, and a shaft of moonlight fell on the man's arm.

Chad stood still, his heart thumping until he was sure he was alone. Then he slowly left the boathouse and walked up the dock. For the first time in a while, he didn't feel so afraid. He'd seen something that might help him find a way out of all this mess.

Chapter Thirty-Five.

"It's a scam," Maria said, rolling her eyes at Gordon in exactly the same way Karen did. It was getting annoying, he thought.

"It's just like getting an email from a Nigerian prince who wants you to send him your bank details so he can send you millions of dollars and then share it with you when he arrives in the country. And you do that, and before you know it, he's stolen $3,652, never to be seen again."

"What?" Gordon said, startled.

Maria picked up her phone and started clicking, suddenly engrossed by the images flickering on her screen.

They were both still in their pyjamas, sitting at the breakfast table by the kitchen window. Gordon liked to watch the hummingbirds buzzing around the feeder that hung outside on their deck. Maria liked to check her Instagram statistics and her followers.

"What do you mean?" Gordon asked again.

Maria waved her hand dismissively and, without looking up, said, "The thing is, Gordy, nobody offers you a million dollars without strings attached."

"Did you send a Nigerian prince $3,652?" he asked.

"No, of course not. Do you think I'm some kind of idiot? Anyway, we're not talking about me; we're talking about you," Maria snapped, this time stopping her scrolling to glare at Gordon.

"Well, the man wasn't offering to give me money," Gordon said, sulking a little at his wife's tone. "He's giving Shell Bay the money."

"What on earth for?" Maria said, looking back down at her phone.

"For whatever the town needs," Gordon said. "Except there are two conditions for the money."

"Aha!" Maria looked up and smiled triumphantly. "I told you. Scammers always want something. Did he ask for bank account numbers?"

"No, he did not." Gordon was irritated now.

"What was his name?" Maria asked. "Did he tell you who he was working for?"

"Of course. I don't deal with people I don't know," Gordon said defensively and mentally rummaged in his brain for the information. Had the man given his name? He was sure he'd asked for it. Never mind, Karen would know.

"Hmm" Maria narrowed her eyes. "So, what did he want? This... man?"

"Two very fair conditions for this special grant, actually. All they asked is that I use some of the money to demolish the old museum and that I support Croud publicly about this murder nonsense. They'll take care of the damn podcaster, they said."

"What museum? I didn't know Shell Bay had a museum. And what podcaster?"

"The old museum at the end of Main Street," Gordon said, ignoring the second question. "Didn't you go there on a school trip?"

Maria shrugged. "I don't remember. But why would he want you to demolish some old museum? That's weird."

It was Gordon's turn to shrug. "I don't know. But the museum has been closed for years. The building is falling apart anyway. No reason why it shouldn't be demolished. He even gave me the name of a contractor they wanted me to use. They said all I had to do was sign off on the grant."

"But then you have to support Croud? I thought you said he was an idiot and just worried about his budget."

"Erm... well, I've thought about it, and you know, he's the expert, and I really shouldn't interfere..."

"Oh, really?" Maria looked sharply at Gordon. "Why did you say all that stuff at the press conference then?"

Gordon shifted uncomfortably in his seat and gazed out the window, hoping to distract Maria by pointing out the hummingbirds.

"Gordon."

"Oh, alright then," Gordon sighed. "It's that damn podcast. Everyone is listening to it, and the whole town is talking about the murder and the talent contest and, you know..." He looked pleadingly at Maria. "Everyone is still laughing at me. I just thought if there was another murder, then people would be distracted and would forget about..." His voice trailed off.

"What podcast are you talking about?"

"Oh, it's called the Shadowcaster Sinister something or other," Gordon grumbled.

Maria tapped at her phone. "Oh, right, I've got it. But look here," she turned her phone around so Gordon could see the screen.

"There's a new episode. And it accuses the police of covering it up, and they call *you* a hero."

"I know," Gordon said. "It was working. The town loves me again. So what do I do? There was something about that man." He fell silent, thinking back to the meeting in his office.

"What about him?"

"I can't put my finger on it," Gordon said. "He was offering me money, which is good, and tearing down the museum makes sense, but he was very firm that the murder investigation should be closed down as soon as possible. It was the way he said it. I just got the impression that he wasn't asking for a favour. It was more 'close down the murder investigation or else'."

"Or else what?" Maria was staring at him.

Gordon shook his head. "I don't know," he admitted. "It was just a feeling."

"And you're sure he didn't give you his name?" Maria pressed.

"No. Oh. He did give me his business card," Gordon said, suddenly remembering that the man had dropped the card on the desk just as he left.

"Do you have it here? If we know who the man is and how to reach him, maybe I can have a chat with him. See if he's legit. I have an instinct for these things."

Gordon took a deep breath and let the relief flood over him. Making decisions wasn't really his thing. "Would you, darling? You always know what's best."

"Of course, my love." Maria reached out and patted Gordon's hand. "I'll see if I can find out more about this podcaster too. I'll chat with the town residents. I've always been a very popular First Lady of Shell Bay. I'm like Oprah to them."

Gordon nodded and got up from the table. "They really do love you," he agreed. "I'll go and get the business card."

Chapter Thirty-Six.

"This is much better," Sarah said, carrying over two mugs of coffee to the table in the corner of The Bean Express and putting one down in front of Jewell and the other in front of the empty seat. "I'll just get the muffins."

When Sarah arrived back with a plate of muffins, Jewell had the manuscript on the table.

"I feel better about looking at it here," Jewell said. "It's safer. I must be getting paranoid, but I feel like somebody is watching me all the time." She shivered.

"Hmm. I feel like that too," Sarah agreed. "Now, let's take a look."

The manuscript was a large bundle of loose-leaf paper, held together by string. The top page was the only one which was printed. The rest were written in the same loopy handwriting as Jewell's card from Charles.

"The Nautilus Circle," Sarah read. "A History of Crime, Corruption, and Greed, by Charles D. Harrington."

"Wow," she said, looking at Jewell. "Heavy stuff."

Sarah felt someone looking over her shoulder.

"Hi there," Alex Harding said. "Got something interesting there?"

"Oh no, just some writing that I've been doing," Sarah lied. "Nothing really."

"It doesn't look like nothing." Alex nodded towards the manuscript, "Looks like a lot of work. I didn't know you were a writer."

"Oh, just a hobby. I'm terrible," Sarah said.

"Well, have fun," Alex said, and moved over to the counter.

Jewell looked at Sarah. "Maybe this wasn't such a good idea," she mumbled.

"Come on, let's read some of this and then we'll go." Sarah shuffled over so Jewell could read the manuscript with her.

They read in silence for half an hour, exchanging the odd glance. Then Jewell whispered, "If even half of this is true, it's no wonder someone wanted to kill Charles. What do we do now?"

"I don't know," Sarah whispered back. "We'll have to hide this and tell nobody until we've decided."

"What are you whispering about?" a voice came from above them. "Are you going to be long? This is my favourite table."

Sarah and Jewell looked up to see Maria Godson, the mayor's wife. She glared down at them. Sarah knew that Maria still held a grudge against her because Sarah had accused her of murdering Commodore Hiscocks. But there was no excuse for rudeness.

Sarah flipped the pages of the manuscript over and said, "We will be as long as we like," but Jewell put a hand on Sarah's arm.

"No problem, Mrs Godson. We are just leaving."

"Are we?"

"Yes," Jewell said firmly.

Sarah saw that Maria Godson was staring at the title page of the manuscript and had her phone in her hand. Sarah scooped it up and put it in her bag.

"All yours," she said, as she and Jewell got up from the table.

When they were outside, Jewell said urgently, "She saw the manuscript. Didn't you see her staring? We've got to be more careful. She takes photos of everything for that stupid Instagram account.

"Don't worry," Sarah said. "I have the perfect hiding place. And Maria Godson had no idea what she was looking at."

Chapter Thirty-Seven.

G ordon Godson was so engrossed in his computer game that he failed to hear raised voices coming from just outside his office.

"Woohoo, survived again," he exclaimed with glee and then looked up as the office door flung open.

"I told you it was a scam," Maria Godson hissed as she barged past Karen into his office.

"Don't mind me," Karen muttered, banging the office door closed, leaving Maria marching over to her husband's desk.

"Didn't I tell you?" Maria demanded as she stood with her hands on her hips, while Gordon sat looking up at her like a deer caught in headlights.

"Baby, you can't just barge in here," he said gently. "I'm in charge of very important, confidential business."

"Oh yes? What are you doing right now?" Maria asked, looking at the open laptop on Gordon's desk. "Is that Minecraft?"

"Never mind," mumbled Gordon, blushing right up to his ears, and closing the laptop with a click. "Now, what is a scam?" he asked.

"That man," Maria snapped. "That man who was telling you some story about giving the city money. Have you forgotten already?"

"Of course not, darling." Gordon said smugly. "And don't worry. I called the number he gave me for the demolition company, and they are completely legit. They had a secretary and everything. They were even expecting my call. That old museum will be a pile of rubble, and all I have to do is to stop Croud from investigating this murder..."

"Darling..."

"Some poor dude, maybe a bit tipsy, falls off the dock, splash, splash, very sad and all that, but..."

"Gordon, shut up!" Maria screeched and slapped the desk.

Gordon jumped in his chair, startled.

"Gordon, look at this," Maria said and pulled her phone out of her purse, tapped the screen, and scrolled. She held out her phone for Gordon to look. "I took this earlier."

He took it off her so he could see what she was showing him. "Ooh, I like it, duck lips, very sexy..."

"Not that one." She snatched the phone back, scrolled again, and handed it to him.

"So? Two women having coffee? What does that mean?" Gordon was confused.

"Zoom in. See what they are looking at?"

Gordon peered closer after enlarging the photo with his thumb and forefinger. "Some document, I think. They're both reading it. But I still..."

"The logo. On the document. Where have you seen that before?"

Gordon recognised it. And with a sinking feeling, knew exactly where he'd seen it before.

Chapter Thirty-Eight

Sarah woke with a start. Her bedclothes were on the floor, and she was shivering. She had a bad dream, and broken fragments were coming back to her as she lay there, the grey light of dawn filtering into her cabin.

In her dream, she was holding something—a bag or a parcel—she wasn't sure, but bad people were trying to get it from her, that much she knew. Their hands were grasping at her, trying to snatch the bag of secrets.

"Bag of secrets," she said out loud.

Of course, it was Charles Harrington's manuscript that had prompted the dream.

"If it's all true," Sarah murmured to herself, and felt a tingle of fear crawl up her spine.

Sarah got up and dressed quickly. She made herself a pot of coffee and stepped out onto the deck of her boat. The September warmth had finally ended, and the morning was gloomy. Sarah felt drizzle in the air, and the dampness clung to her face and hair.

Sarah shivered. It wasn't just the chill, she thought. It was something else. The feeling of being watched. The feeling had been with her for a couple of days. She'd put it down to the aftermath of Charles' murder and now the discovery of the manuscript. She was just being paranoid.

Sarah decided to check on Jewell. They had to decide what to do with the manuscript. Sarah was ready to hand it over to Linda and the police. What else would they do with it? Publish it? Put themselves in the same danger as Charles? No, it was better to give it to the police, and they could investigate if they believed any of it. Now that Agnes Crofton had been abducted, they surely couldn't ignore it, could they?

Sarah walked across the marina and stepped onto Jewell's boat. Strange, she thought. The cabin door was open, just a crack. Maybe Jewell was up and about already. She'd probably had a sleepless night too.

"Jewell," Sarah called. "Are you up?"

She stepped forward and called again, this time a little louder. Then she pulled the cabin door open.

"Jewell? Are you...?"

She froze and her hand flew to her mouth. "Oh no," she whispered. The cabin was pulled apart. Cushions, drawers, cutlery, clothes, all of Jewell's possessions were scattered around the galley and cabin. The door to Jewell's stateroom was open, but Jewell wasn't there. There was just the mattress pulled off the bed, and cupboard doors hanging open.

She stopped herself from going further into the cabin. A voice in her mind told her not to touch anything. She started to back out, and then she noticed something on the floor.

"No, no..." She moaned. There was a small pool of something dark red. Instantly, Sarah had a flashback to finding Commodore Hiscocks lying dead in a pool of blood. She was back there, the metallic smell mixed with burnt coffee... then she was back in the present.

Smell. There was a smell in this cabin. Not blood. Something else. What was it?

Sarah gave herself a shake. What was she doing? She had to get the police here now. They had to find Jewell. Sarah glanced once more at the blood on the floor of the cabin before she left, hoping it wasn't too late for Jewell.

Chapter Thirty-Nine.

Linda arrived at work early. She avoided going to The Bean Express. She felt like a coward, but she had no news for Natalie, and it seemed frivolous, somehow, to be buying muffins when Agnes was out there, waiting to be rescued. At least that's what Linda hoped. She couldn't bring herself to think about the alternative scenario.

So Linda made coffee in the office and stood in the conference room, gazing at the whiteboard and trying to make sense of it all. Were there connections between all these strange occurrences? Was she trying to fit together pieces that just didn't go together?

"Start with the basics, Linda," she muttered, and she paced slowly around the room, speaking out loud as if she were *Miss Marple* addressing the gathered suspects in an English village murder.

"To start, we have a very dead Charles D. Harrington. The evidence, a skull with a bullet hole in it, points to murder. Jewell Winslow tells us that Charles believed he was in danger, and she thought it had something to do with his work. Jewell also says she saw shadowy figures struggling on the dock about the time that Charles ended up in the water. But then the skull goes missing, the coroner disappears, and the CCTV at the dock shows... nothing. Not only that, there is no sign of any manuscript. Nobody at Sea Breeze Marina saw or heard anything except Jewell."

Linda paused to let her imaginary audience process the information.

"It appears, ladies and gentlemen, that either there was no murder, or someone—or some people—are trying very hard to make sure Charles Harrington's death is not investigated.

"And then we come to the disappearance of Agnes Crofton," she continued, waving her hand for the invisible, yet enthralled crowd. "A disagreeable gossip who knows everything that happens in the small town of Shell Bay. She too, is behaving strangely, just before her abduction—if that is what it is—and her house is turned upside down. Somebody is looking for something. Something incriminating maybe? Did Agnes know too much?

"And then there is the strange tale of Agnes Crofton's mother, Eliza, who also died under mysterious circumstances. So what connects these strange occurrences? The mysterious Nautilus Circle just as Agnes believed? Because I very much believe, ladies and gentlemen, that there *is* a connection, and what's more, I intend to prove it and find the killer."

And with that, Linda made a theatrical flourish with her hands and gave a deep bow.

A slow handclap from the doorway made Linda jump.

"Bravo," Wenda said drily. "Sorry to interrupt your... performance, but there is a hysterical woman in reception asking for you."

"Who?"

"I don't... oh hang on." Wenda disappeared, and Linda could hear muffled voices. Then she reappeared. "The mayor's in reception too," she announced. "He is also hysterical. You have to come and deal with them. This is too early for me to be bothered with all this."

"Alright, I'm coming." Linda sighed. She really needed to focus on these cases, connected or not, without distractions.

"Did you get muffins?" Wenda asked as Linda followed her out to reception.

"No."

"Geez, what a terrible start to the day."

"Alright, calm down, Sarah," Linda said, resting her hand on the older woman's shoulder. She could see that Sarah was valiantly trying not to cry.

"Take deep breaths."

Sarah did that, and in a few moments was able to get words out.

"Jewell is gone." Sarah's voice lowered as if afraid someone was listening. "There's blood on her boat. Someone must think we found the manuscript."

Linda stared at her. "Did you?"

Sarah nodded. "And I have to tell you what was in it—m" she began, but was interrupted.

"Don't believe a word that woman says," the mayor blustered behind them. "She's trying to make me look like an idiot."

"Wenda, would you show Mayor Godson to Staff Sergeant Croud's office, please?" Linda asked.

"Oh, alright," Wenda rolled her eyes. "Come on, mayor."

"But that woman, she is a scam artist," the mayor protested, but did follow Wenda out of the reception area. "She and her friend sent a very intimidating man to my office..." His voice faded away.

"What was he talking about?" Linda asked Sarah. "Why does he think you're a scammer?"

"I have no idea."

Linda shook her head. "That man doesn't need anyone to make him look like an idiot. He does that all by himself."

She pointed to a chair. "Let me get my purse, and some gloves and tape. I'll come and check Jewell's boat, and then you can tell me all about the manuscript, okay?"

Just as Linda was collecting her purse from her desk, Constable Reynolds wandered into the office.

"Morning, Sarge," he said with a grin. "What's up with the mayor? Something about a scammer? Did a Nigerian prince rip him off then?"

"Probably," Linda smirked, "but I don't have time to find out."

She quickly told Ray what was going on. "Holy crap," he muttered and then his eyes widened. "Oh Sarge, I forgot."

"What?"

"You know you asked me to check Agnes Crofton's phone records? Well, they came through yesterday evening after you left."

"Anything interesting?"

"Yes, Sarge, something very interesting indeed."

Chapter Forty.

"Charles Harrington called Agnes?" Linda repeated.

"Yes, Sarge. Twice. First time was less than a minute, so he probably left a message, and then the second call was ten minutes."

"So we can definitely prove the connection between Agnes and Harrington." Linda closed her eyes briefly, and in her mind heard her imaginary audience from earlier, giving her a standing ovation.

"This changes everything," Linda said. "Even without the physical evidence of foul play, it will be easier to establish that Charles Harrington must have been murdered. Now that Agnes and Jewell have both disappeared, the two people with direct connections to the victim, there is no possible way that his death was a tragic accident. And the phone call corroborates Natalie's story."

"Looks that way, Sarge," Ray said. "What do we do now?"

"You stay here and re-work the board. Let's find all the connections we can between all three victims. Anything at all to strengthen our case. And I'll go to Jewell's boat and see what I can find. We'll get forensics out there and see if we can get anything that matches any evidence from Agnes' house."

"Righto, Sarge."

Linda snapped on a pair of latex gloves.

"Stay here, Sarah," she said. "I don't want the crime scene contaminated. Where did you see the blood?"

"In the cabin," Sarah said. "On the galley floor. It's a real mess in there. The cabin door was open when I got here, but I did close it when I left."

"Right."

Linda stepped onto the deck of The Little Gem, and the boat rocked slightly. "Was there anything else unusual?" she asked. "Apart from the obvious mess and Jewell not being here, I mean. Did you see anyone leave the boat, or was there anyone hanging around?"

"No, nothing. Except..." Sarah bit her lip.

"Except what, Sarah? Anything, no matter how insignificant it seems, might be important, so spit it out." Linda didn't mean to sound impatient, but Sarah hadn't noticed.

"It's just that there was a... smell," Sarah said. "It was familiar, but I don't know where from. I've smelled it before. I even thought I smelled it on my boat. Just a slight waft. There and then gone."

"Was it aftershave?" Linda asked.

"No, it was more like a chemical," Sarah said. "I don't know. It's been bothering me."

Linda left Sarah waiting on the dock. With her gloved hand, she opened the cabin door and surveyed the mess. Every cupboard door was open, and the contents of drawers were scattered everywhere. Cushions had been pulled off the chairs and ripped open, so small tufts of stuffing were resting on everything, as if there had been a snowstorm in the tiny galley. Linda saw the pool of blood on the floor, just as Sarah had described.

She moved slowly into the cabin, being careful where she stepped, so as not to disturb evidence. The forensic team would not thank her for messing up the crime scene. The door to Jewell's stateroom was open, and Linda could see the mattress was halfway pulled off the bunk, and Jewell's clothes were flung haphazardly around the tiny room.

There wasn't much that Linda could do, she decided, until the crime scene techs had processed the scene.

She moved two steps back and then stopped. What was that? Linda sniffed. Sarah was right. There was an unmistakable smell.

Something clicked in her brain. That smell, it had been in Agnes' house, after the break-in. It was sickly, and cloying, and hung in the air like a heavy chemical. Whatever or whoever made or carried that smell had been on this boat and in Agnes' house.

Then it came to her, like a lightbulb switching on. She knew exactly where she'd smelled that odour before.

"Damn it," Linda cursed under her breath. Ray Reynolds would never let her forget this.

Chapter Forty-One.

Linda and Ray watched Chad Garner through the glass window of the interview room.

He was sitting at the interview table. His head was jerking from side to side, and his lips were moving as if he were practicing answers to potential interview questions. The way he stuck out his chest and gestured with his chin reminded Linda of a cocky little Bantam hen.

"I told you he was trouble, Sarge," Ray said.

Linda glared at him, hearing the tiny note of triumph in the Constable's voice.

"You did, Constable," Linda acknowledged, "and I didn't take the warning seriously. I'm sorry."

"That's okay, Sarge." Ray grinned. "Everyone makes mistakes, right? We're all human."

"Let's move on, shall we?" Linda said irritably. "Let's make sure this arrogant piece of work is squirming by the end of this interview, right?"

When Linda and Ray had found Chad, he was puffing away on his vape, leaning up against the door of the boathouse, next to the marina office.

They had both smelled the vape smoke before they got to him. It was the same scent that had lingered in Agnes' home and Jewell's boat.

Chad had seen Linda and Ray approaching, and if he was worried, he didn't show it.

"How's it going, Deputy?" he grinned. "Oh, sorry, Constable," and he chuckled before sucking on his vape stick and blowing out a cloud of smoke that hung in the air.

"Is that it, Sarge?" Ray had asked, waving his hand in the air and dispersing the smoke.

"It is indeed, Constable," Linda had replied. "Exactly the same."

"What?" Chad was still smiling. "What are you two on about?"

"I'll take that," Linda said briskly and snatched the vape out of Chad's hand before he had time to react.

"Hey! Give that back. You can't do that. There's no law against—" He was almost yelling now.

"Evidence," Linda interrupted, taking out a bag from her pocket and dropping the vape into it.

"Right then," she said to Chad, "you are coming with us. You're going to tell us all about Agnes Crofton and Jewell Winslow."

"No idea what you're talking about," Chad sneered, "and I ain't going with you. You'll have to arrest me first."

"Fair enough," Linda smiled brightly. "Constable Reynolds, please read Mr Garner his rights."

Chad Garner had protested and shouted, and made quite the scene as Linda and Ray led him up the ramp and pushed him in the back of the police cruiser. They had ignored his questions and insults, all the way back to the detachment where they put him in an interview room until he'd quietened down.

Ray nodded his head at Chad sitting in the room. "He's nervous. See his leg?"

Linda did. Despite Chad's defiant posture, underneath the table, one of his legs was jiggling up and down. It was a physical giveaway to his nervousness.

She grinned. "Are you ready for this? Good cop, bad cop, Ray?"

"No, Sarge," he said seriously. "Bad cop, bad cop."

Linda and Ray strode into the interview room. Linda was carrying a file, and she slapped it down on the table in front of Chad.

"Ooooh, scary," Chad smirked at her.

Linda ignored him. She and Ray took their seats. They both sat back with their arms folded, staring at Chad in silence.

At first, Chad mimicked the way they were sitting. He stared back, a wide grin on his face.

After two whole minutes, the grin faded.

"Get on with it then," he said. "Ask away. You can't keep me here forever."

Linda and Ray didn't move or say anything.

"Oh, I get it," Chad said. "This is a wind-up, right? You two think you can scare me. That's funny, that is." And the grin reappeared.

Linda let another minute go by. Then she turned to Ray. "Constable, what time is it?"

Ray made a big show of pulling out his phone and checking the screen. "It's 3:23 pm, Sarge."

"Thank you, Constable. Just seven minutes before he arrives then."

Ray nodded, but his eyes were still on Chad.

"Is everything in place?" Linda asked.

"Yes, Sarge. He'll arrive at 3:30 pm and walk past the interview room after that."

"So, he'll get a good look in here, right?"

"Yes, Sarge, he will."

Chad's head was swiveling back and forth as if he were watching a tennis match during this exchange. His grin was gone.

"Who are you talking about?" he demanded. "What's all this? Who will be looking in here?"

Linda looked at Ray. "Shall I tell him, or do you want to?"

"If it's okay with you, Sarge, I'd like to."

"Go ahead, Constable." Linda waved her hand, gesturing her agreement.

Ray leaned forward and placed his large hands on the table. In a loud stage whisper, he said, "We've arrested Big Normy for the assault and abduction of Jewell Winslow."

Linda bit her lip and turned her head away so Chad wouldn't see her amusement.

"Whaaattt?" Chad's eyes widened in confusion. "But isn't that why I'm here? Because you wanna pin that on me?"

Ray leaned back and refolded his arms. "That's the thing, Chad. You're just here for a chat. But Big Normy doesn't know that, does he?"

Chad stiffened. "You're bluffing," he muttered, but there was a note of uncertainty in his voice. "You've got nothing on Big Normy."

Ray looked at Linda. "Have we, Sarge?"

Linda shrugged. "We might, and then we might not. All we're doing is chatting to 'persons of interest' who might or might not be able to point the finger at the perpetrator of this heinous crime."

Now Linda leaned forward, mirroring Ray's position. "You see, Chad, we only need one rat to talk, and all the other vermin to know about it."

"Just a few minutes more, Chad, and then you can go. If you have nothing to tell us."

Instantly, Chad's face crumpled, and his shoulders hunched. His cocky attitude dissipated, and he transformed into a scared, immature teenager in front of their eyes.

"Alright, alright," Chad said, looking wildly from Linda and Ray to the interview room door. "It was me. I did it. Please don't arrest Big Normy. I'm not a rat, I'm not, please don't—"

Ray lifted his hand to stop Chad from talking.

"Here's what we can do for you, Chad. If you tell us everything - the truth, mind, then I'll make sure that our receptionist apologises to Big Normy and tells him we made a mistake. But if you mess us about..."

Chad shook his head vigorously. "I won't mess you about. I'll tell you everything I know, I promise, just please..." His eyes went once more to the door.

Ray sighed and got up with a grunt. He ambled to the door and opened it.

"Please hurry." Chad's voice was a high-pitched squeak.

Linda watched Ray leave the room.

"Right now, Mr Garner," she said, opening her file and pulling out a pen from her pocket. "While we are waiting for Constable Reynolds to join us again, why don't we start with some basic information?"

With his bottom lip trembling, Chad Garner started to talk.

Chapter Forty-Two

C had Garner confessed to breaking into Agnes Crofton's house and Jewell's boat and assaulting both women," Linda said, standing at the front of the conference room and pointing to the whiteboard, which now had a photograph of a sullen-faced Chad stuck in the middle. "But he refuses to tell us where they are or if they are dead or alive. He says he was told to break in, knock them around a bit, and then leave. After that, he claims he doesn't know what happened. He just got told what to do and was in fear for his life, apparently."

"So they could be dead and buried somewhere," Ray said bluntly, "and Chad Garner is spinning us a story."

"The evidence doesn't point to either of them being killed at either crime scene," Linda said, pointing at the photographs of Agnes' kitchen and Jewell's galley. "See? There's not enough blood. This part is consistent with Chad's story."

Linda and Ray both stared at the board, which was covered with photographs and notes.

"The thing is," Linda said, "if Chad did hit them and knock them out, how would he have moved them without being seen? He has no car, and he's not a big guy. I don't think he's strong enough to get them very far. If they were knocked out, they would have been dead weights. I just don't see it."

"So you believe him? You think Chad was getting set up?" Ray asked.

"Either he's working with someone, or he's being set up by someone. He's definitely dumb enough. Everything points to Chad being the perpetrator, right? Who breaks in, hits old ladies, and then leaves? And when he's caught, he makes up this ridiculous story about a faceless man forcing him to do dirty deeds by threatening his life. Sounds far-fetched, right?"

"Except there's everything else going on," Linda continued. "The death of Charles Harrington, the missing evidence, the missing manuscript, the story about the death of Harrington's father and Agnes Crofton's mother and father, the call that Harrington made to Agnes just before she disapp eared..."

"And that damn podcaster making a mockery of us and this investigation." Croud's voice came from behind them.

Linda and Ray turned to look at the Staff Sergeant as he stepped into the room.

"The mayor's waiting in my office," he said. "I need you to bring me up to date." He gestured at the whiteboard. "He thinks he's been the victim of a scam, and he won't go until he's got some answers. He's driving me mad. Where are we with this mess?"

Linda walked him through the investigation, right from the beginning. Croud listened intently without interrupting.

"So you think this manuscript that Harrington was working on—you think it's key to the investigation?" he asked. "You're sure it's not some conspiracy theory cooked up by the podcaster idiot?"

Linda shook her head. "I don't know how Shadowcaster knew about the manuscript," she said, "but we now have a connection between Agnes and Harrington. He called her just before he died. And it was obvious that whoever took Agnes was looking for something, and it looks that way on Jewell's boat too."

"Whoever is feeding this podcaster fellow with all this information is to blame," Croud said grimly. "When I find out who it is and who this podcaster idiot is, I will throw the book at both of them."

"Do you think this Nautilus Circle has anything to do with it?" Ray asked. "Or is it just some conspiracy that Agnes believed all her life?"

Linda shook her head. "I don't know. But I am sure Charles Harrington believed it, and I'm sure it's what his manuscript is all about. Someone with influence forced Shirley Grimm into retirement and tried to tamper with evidence."

"Do you think it's the podcaster?" Ray asked. His voice came out as a croak, and he cleared his throat. Linda looked at him sharply. Ray almost sounded....nervous?

"It might be," she said. "Either way, the podcaster has a lot to answer for. He broadcast key details of the investigation and possibly put Agnes and Jewell in danger."

Ray looked away. Linda was about to ask him if there was anything wrong when Wenda's voice broke in.

"That woman's back again. What shall I tell her?"

"Please ask her to wait or come back later," Linda said. "I'll update her when—"

"So you don't want that book thingy she has then?" Wenda interrupted. "It's all wet and covered with seaweed..."

Linda pushed past her and headed out to the reception.

"Sorry," Sarah said, holding up a sopping wet plastic bag draped with fronds of green seaweed. "I forgot to give it to you. It's the manuscript. I put it in a crab trap and hung it off my boat. For safekeeping," she added.

"It must be 900 pages long, Sarge," Ray said, looking at Harrington's manuscript, which Linda placed on the conference table.

"The Nautilus Circle," he read aloud. "A History of Corruption, Crime and Greed, by Charles D. Harrington."

There was a design on the first page, a shell surrounded by stars. Linda looked at it and felt a glimmer of recognition. Where had she seen that before?

Ray flicked over the first page and continued, "Dedicated to the victims: Eliza and Henry Crofton, and Douglas Harrington. RIP."

Ray turned back the page. "What now?"

"Yes, what now?" Croud demanded. "How does this help us find our two missing victims?"

Before Linda could reply, Mayor Godson walked into the conference room. "Croud, how much longer are you going to be? Have you arrested that woman yet? She made a complete fool of me... Hey, what have you got there?"

He pointed to the manuscript. "That's the same logo as this." He stuck his hand in his pocket and pulled out a business card. He dropped it on the table beside the manuscript.

Linda picked it up and turned it over. It read 'The Nautilus Circle', but there was no address or telephone number.

"Where did you get this?" she demanded.

The mayor coloured up and answered defensively, "If you must know, from a charity or something who are giving us a grant for a new museum."

"What? Where are the contact details?"

The mayor shrugged. "They will contact me as soon as the old museum is demolished."

Croud cut in. "I don't understand. Somebody who didn't leave proper contact details is giving you a grant? With no paperwork? How is that proper procedure?"

The mayor's face went a deeper red. "It's all aboveboard," he said. "Well, not completely, but all I had to do was promise to demolish the museum and put a stop to the murder investigation, and then they would transfer the cash." He paused. "What?"

He looked around at the faces of Linda, Ray, and Croud, who were staring at him. "What's the matter? It's all for the good of the town, and you said yourself, Croud, murder investigations are expensive, and we need a museum, don't we? And they even arranged for the demolition. Should be started today." The mayor looked expectantly at the room. "I did good, didn't I?"

Croud spluttered, "You took a bribe, that's what you did. It's not good at all, mayor."

"Wait." A lightbulb pinged in Linda's brain. "The museum." She ran to her desk and grabbed the box that Natalie had given her. She rummaged in it for the photograph of Eliza and Henry Crofton standing beside Douglas Harrington.

She brought it back to the conference room. "See here," she said, "they are standing in front of the museum."

Linda turned the photograph over and read, "Eliza Crofton, Curator of Shell Bay Museum, 1942-1965."

"So?" Croud asked. "What does that mean?"

"The Nautilus Circle wants the museum destroyed," Linda said. "It must be for a reason. Maybe they think the manuscript is there?"

Linda turned to the mayor. "When did you say the museum would be demolished?"

"Right now," he said. "Why?"

"Sir," Linda said urgently. "I think I know where Agnes and Jewell are being held."

Chapter Forty-Three.

Something brushed against Jewell's cheek. It was enough to wake her up. She tried to move her hand to her face. She hated moths, and that's what it felt like, a moth brushing gently against her face.

Her hand didn't move. She tried again, but her hand stubbornly refused to move.

What was happening? Was she dreaming? She'd had dreams like this before when she'd been frozen. Jewell concentrated on waking up.

Then she heard a grunt. No, impossible. But this was starting to feel all wrong. Her bed felt as hard as a rock. Did she fall asleep on the floor? Was she drunk last night? As soon as that thought popped into her head, Jewell felt a pounding pain behind her eyes and noticed the metallic taste in her mouth.

"Arrgh," she said and licked her very dry lip. That was it. She'd drunk way too much last night and somehow passed out on the floor instead of her bed. Dear God, she hadn't done this since...

"Ooooarrrgggghhh!"

The sound came from behind her.

Was it Joseph? Sarah? Had they all gotten drunk together?

Jewell struggled to move. Why couldn't she move? And that was something else. Why was it so dark and silent? No gulls calling, no waves lapping against the side of the boat...

The boat.

Fragments of a memory formed in her mind. She was on her boat, in the galley. The boat rocked a little, and she looked around and saw... who? Jewell remembered the flicker of recognition she'd felt, but not the face. It would come back to her. Right now, she had other problems.

Jewell sat up and then collapsed again. Her hands were behind her back, and now that she was fully awake, she could feel tight rope or cord cutting into her wrists. She couldn't move her legs either; her ankles were bound together.

"Oh no, oh no," Jewell muttered as the memory of the previous night returned in full. This was not good, she thought. Not good at all.

Someone had hit her on the head. And now she was tied up... but where was she? Fear bubbled up at the back of her throat and made her whimper.

"Ooooarrrghhh!" The sound came again.

Jewell realised she wasn't alone. "Who's there?" she whispered, afraid it might be the same person who'd hit her and tied her up.

A hiccuping sound echoed in the darkness.

With a huge effort, Jewell lifted her knees to her chest and rolled over on her side. Her eyes were adjusting to the darkness. She could just make out a dark hump. It moved and made another noise.

"AARRRGGGGG!"

This time, it was louder.

Whoever it was, Jewell decided, they must be bound and gagged.

"Hello," she said and was surprised at how raspy her voice was. "I hope you're friendly?"

"Oooorrrggg," the hump replied, and Jewell was certain she saw a head nod up and down.

"My hands are tied behind my back," Jewell said, as softly as possible because who knows who might be listening? "Are yours? Just grunt once for yes."

The grunt came.

"We need to be back to back," Jewell continued in her hoarse whisper. "Then we might be able to untie each other. I am going to shuffle over to you. Is that okay?"

Another grunt came in the darkness.

Jewell took a deep breath, and then wiggled her body, using her feet to gain purchase on the floor. It was a slow, laborious process, and Jewell imagined she must look like a lumpy snake, putting her feet in front of her and then straining every muscle to force her torso to follow.

The floor was uneven and hard, and Jewell hoped there wasn't anything sharp that would cut her, but all she seemed to encounter was grit and dust.

Eventually, Jewell was close enough to the hump to see it was another woman, her dark eyes glinting with fear in the darkness. Jewell kept on shuffling until they were face to face.

"Now we need to turn over, so we can untie each other," Jewell said quietly. "Are you ready?"

The head in front of her nodded.

With more grunts and groans, both captives turned their bodies over so they were back to back.

Jewell could feel the back of the other woman with her bound hands. Jewell wiggled some more and then touched fingers.

"Right, I will work on your hands first," she said, and with her nimble fingers, used to working with rope during all her boating days, touched the rope that bound the other woman's hands.

Inwardly thankful that the kidnapper had used some kind of nylon twine and not plastic zip ties, Jewell went to work on the knots.

"Granny knot," she snorted, and in a few minutes had eased the knot loose, and then felt the rope go slack.

Jewell felt the other woman sit up, and then a moment later, heard her cough.

Then there were fingers working on the rope that bound Jewell, and again, moments later, Jewell felt the tightness lessen around her wrists, and her hands were free.

Gingerly, Jewell sat up and turned around to face the other woman.

"Are you all right?" she asked, shocked to see Agnes Croften sitting there.

Agnes nodded her head. "I don't suppose," her husky voice whispered hopefully, "that you have any cigarettes?"

Chapter Forty-Four.

Ernie Fletcher cursed as scrambled egg mixed with whatever fancy spicy sauce was in the newfangled breakfast thingy he'd just purchased from a rude girl at the only coffee shop in town, dropped down his plaid shirt, and landed in his lap, leaving a shiny stain on his work pants. He rubbed at it with the paper bag it came in and instantly made it worse.

He cursed again.

He hadn't wanted this wrap thing. He wanted to buy something warm and greasy, like a sausage roll or a sweet muffin to go with the large coffee, which, admittedly, was very good.

"No sausage rolls," the girl had said.

"One of those muffins then?" Ernie had pointed at a rack of muffins with drizzles of caramel sauce and nut sprinkles behind the girl. They were still warm because he'd watched the girl use oven mitts to carry out the rack. The warm, chocolaty caramel smell was making his stomach growl.

"All sold," the girl said.

"What?" Ernie was sure he'd heard incorrectly.

The girl took a deep breath and then sighed theatrically, rolling her eyes for extra emphasis, "I said, all the muffins are sold."

"That can't be right..." Ernie squinted at the girl's name badge. "Natalie. It's 7:30, you just opened. How can all the muffins be sold?" He took a slow, deliberate look around the cafe. "I am your first customer. There's nobody else here."

Just then, the door opened, and the bell jingled.

A man walked into the cafe whistling cheerfully. Natalie glared at Ernie, who waved the other man to the counter. "You go ahead," Ernie said, "I'm still deciding."

"Morning, Nat," the man said, smiling and nodding his thanks to Ernie. "Coffee and a muffin, please."

"No problem." Natalie poured a coffee and popped a warm muffin in a paper bag. "That'll be $5.50."

Ernie watched the man pay before he left the cafe with his coffee and muffin.

"Have you decided yet?" Natalie asked in a bored tone.

"Yes, I'd like a coffee and muffin, please," Ernie repeated, unable to keep the irritation out of his voice.

"I told you already. Muffins are all sold. Are you deaf?"

"No, I'm not bloody... you just sold that guy a muffin," Ernie exploded.

Natalie's expression didn't change. She gestured at a small sign on the counter.

"World Famous Mocha Chocha Crunch Muffins must be ordered 24 hours in advance."

"Told you," Natalie said smugly, folding her arms across her chest. "All. The. Muffins. Are. Sold." She said the words slowly, as if she were talking to a small child.

"Fine." Ernie was too hungry to argue. "What *do* you have?"

"Breakfast Wrap."

"Give me one of those and a coffee. Please," he added.

"For here or to go?"

"To go."

"You need room in your coffee?"

Ernie blinked. "What?"

Natalie sighed again. "You want me to leave room in the cup for milk or cream?"

"No. I take my coffee black."

"Coming right up.".

"World famous muffins, my ass," Ernie muttered under his breath as Natalie turned away to fill a cardboard cup with black coffee. "I've never heard of 'em."

Half an hour later, Ernie was sitting in the cab of his excavator, cursing about his lukewarm coffee and gloopy breakfast wrap.

The day had got off to a bad start. First, Gary, his boss, had phoned early in the morning with this rush job. Second, Ernie's son had already gone to work, so Ernie had to load the excavator on his flatbed truck, all by himself. Then, it had taken an extra half hour to find Shell Bay, and then there was that girl in the cafe.

Gary wouldn't pay for Ernie's travel time, only the time he was on site, and judging by the state of this old wooden building, Ernie could have given it one good shove with his shoulder, and it would have fallen down. It would only take him three hours tops to have it pulverised into a pile of splintered planks.

Ernie settled back into his seat and closed his eyes. He'd have a quick nap before he started. He was going to log eight hours for this job, no matter what.

Chapter Forty-Five.

"What happened to you?" Jewell asked Agnes.

They were in a basement of some kind, or a storage shed. It was windowless, but light filtered in through cracks in the walls, so the two women were able to assess their surroundings. They had moved cautiously around, feeling their way around boxes and broken furniture in the shadows, looking for a way out. They had found one door, but it was locked, and even though they both used the last of their strength to try and break it down, it wouldn't budge.

Now they were slumped on the floor, drained of all energy and desperate for a drink of water.

"I was hit over the head," Agnes croaked. "I heard a car outside, thought it was Linda coming home. Before I knew it, I heard someone rushing up behind me, and wham, hit me, and I woke up here. What about you?"

"Same, sort of. Except I got a look at him before he hit me."

"You did?"

"Yes, it was Chad Garner. He works at the marina, doing odd jobs and maintenance."

"So why hit you? Was he robbing you?"

Jewell was silent for a minute. "I think he was looking for something."

Agnes was quiet too. "Jewell, what was he looking for?"

Jewell told her about the manuscript.

In the gloom, she could see Agnes nod her head. "Then Chad works for some very dangerous people."

"Are they going to kill us?" Jewell asked, unable to hide the tremor in her voice.

"I think so."

Just then, they heard a rumbling sound, and the ground shook, dust coating them. The vibration continued, and soon bits of lumber and objects were falling and hitting the concrete floor.

They heard the creak of wood splintering.

"We need to move," Agnes croaked.

"Where?" Jewell whimpered. "Where can we go?"

Agnes got to her feet and grabbed Jewell. "Into the corner," she said, loud enough for Jewell to hear over the roar of an engine.

Linda was driving the police cruiser with Ray beside her. Croud was following.

"Sirens on," she shouted at Ray. She hoped that Croud had ordered the mayor to get city workers over to the museum as quickly as possible.

Maybe they would be in time to stop the demolition. But as Linda rounded the corner and caught sight of the derelict building, there was an excavator with its heavy iron claw pounding the roof of the museum.

Linda punched the brakes and brought the cruiser to a halt. "Keep the sirens and lights going," she ordered Ray and then got out.

Surely the operator could see the police lights? But the claw kept pounding, and then its iron jaws opened, and it scooped up a pile of crushed lumber.

Linda stood and waved her arms, screaming at the excavator, but she could see the operator had large earmuffs on, and the cab was facing in the opposite direction.

"What do we do?" Ray was beside her, and Linda was dimly aware of Croud's car pulling up behind them.

Ray and Linda jumped up and down and shouted, but their voices were drowned out by the noise.

"It's no use," Linda cried and took off running towards the excavator.

"Sarge!" she heard Ray shout, but she didn't look back.

Chapter Forty-Six

The excavator groaned to a stop, the heavy metal claw clamped around museum debris like a metal fistful of twigs.

The operator, a red-faced bald man, was pulling off his furry headphones and shouting at Linda. "What are you doing? You can't be up here. It's dangerous. You might have been killed, you silly..."

He stopped when Linda, panting from running and climbing up the side of it to the cab, released one of her hands from gripping the cab door and dug in her pocket for her warrant card, shoving it towards his face.

"Police? What's going on?"

"There are people in that building," Linda bellowed. "You have to stop tearing it down, *now.*"

"What? People? But it was chained up when I got here," the man said, his ruddy face getting paler. "I checked. And who would be in there? Homeless people? Oh, my God..."

He and Linda stared at the half-demolished museum. The front end of it was smashed to pieces. The roof truss was creaking precariously, and the sides of the wooden building, which were still standing, bulged as if they were about to give way.

Linda glanced down at the ground, where Croud, the mayor, and Ray Reynolds were looking at the wreck in horror. Then, just as the roof truss made an ominous groan and dipped further towards the ground, Linda watched as Constable Ray Reynolds rubbed his face and tilted his head from side to side as if readying for a fight, and then took off running as fast as he could towards the crumbling building.

"Ray," Linda screamed, but her voice was lost in the breeze. She looked down to see Croud running around in circles like a half-crazed crow, shouting after Ray as the constable disappeared into the rubble.

"What is that bloody idiot doing?" the operator cried out in alarm. "He'll get himself killed."

"Just stay put," Linda hissed. "Don't move this damn machine an inch."

"Am I in trouble?" The man was agitated. "I had no idea; how could I know? I was just sent here to do this job; it was given the all-clear..."

"Who sent you?" Linda demanded. "Who do you work for?"

"I work for myself," the man said. "I do work for all sorts..."

"But who sent you to this job, dammit?"

"Oh, I dunno, probably Binns Salvage and Waste. He usually gets the city jobs..."

In a second, Linda was scrambling down to the ground and running towards Croud. "It's Gary Binns," she gasped. "At the marina. They sent the excavator. And Binns has tattoos on his arm. I saw the logo on his laptop. It makes sense."

"Go, go," Croud said urgently. "I've got ambulances and construction trucks on the way. We'll get Ray out of there."

As Linda raced away from the museum towards the police cruiser, she heard a loud cracking and groaning of splitting wood, like a tree falling in the forest, and then a thump and crash as the roof of the museum finally caved in.

As Linda scrambled into the cruiser, turned her key in the ignition, and screeched away towards the marina, she heard the distant sound of sirens coming closer.

She just hoped they weren't too late.

Chapter Forty-Seven

The police cruiser skidded to a halt, kicking up gravel in the marina parking lot. Linda was out of the car, running down the ramp a second later.

Fiona Driver was standing on the dock.

"Detective Sergeant, what's going..." she started as Linda ran towards her. The dock was swaying slightly from Linda's frantic movement.

"The Binns, are they still here?" Linda gasped, slowing down.

"They've just paid up and given notice. They're leaving now," Fiona said, bewildered. "If you are quick, you'll catch them."

Linda raced on to see Gary Binns untying the Goodfellas and then hopping on the stern. Linda could smell the diesel engine, and the propeller was churning in the water.

"Gary Binns. Stop right there. Police," she bellowed.

She saw Gary glance in her direction, then he climbed into the wheel-house just as Linda arrived at the dock beside the boat.

The engine roared some more, and Linda realised that Binns was about to push the throttle forward and take off. Alison Binns was in the wheelhouse with her husband, shouting and waving her hands for him to get a move on.

"Here goes." Linda didn't give herself time to think before she took the leap from the dock, over the rapidly expanding gap of water, to the stern of the Goodfellas.

She hit the deck and collapsed into a heap, just as Gary pushed the lever so the engine went from idling to full throttle.

The boat jerked and shuddered, and Linda reached out for something to grab and steady herself. Her hand found the rail above the stern, and she dragged herself to her feet.

Alison Binns was red-faced and screaming at her, but Linda couldn't hear a thing over the roar of the engine. What should she do now?

Linda vaguely realised that jumping onto the boat was a dumb idea. She had no weapon, no way of making Binns stop the boat and return to the dock. Given the look on Alison Binn's face as she charged towards Linda, showing a warrant card and reading the woman her rights was unlikely to resolve the situation either.

Linda glanced over her shoulder and saw Fiona standing on the dock, just beside where the Goodfellas had been moored. The wake of the boat was making the docks rock and roll, and Linda could just see the con-sternation on Fiona's face. She hoped the marina manager would have the presence of mind to call the Coastguard.

"What are you doing on our boat, you... you... stowaway," Alison Binns hissed as she launched herself towards Linda.

"I'm police, I can..." Linda managed to get out before the short, stocky woman, with bleach-blonde hair flying, collided with Linda, sending her sprawling on the deck once more.

"Don't be an idiot," Linda gasped. "I'm a police officer," and then, just as she caught sight of Alison Binn's crimson nails, Linda turned her head and felt the talons scrape her cheek.

Alison was on top of Linda now, clawing and tugging on handfuls of Linda's hair, which made her cry out and tears of pain stream down her face. Alison was a short woman, but she was bulky enough to have pushed the air out of Linda's lungs when she slammed into her.

Out of the corner of Linda's eyes, through the blur of her tears, she caught sight of a blue handle. It looked like a pole of some sort.

Linda strained to move her arm out straight, and then her fingers closed around the pole. With as much force as she could muster, she brought it down across Alison Binn's back.

It obviously didn't hurt that much, because Alison just let out a yelp, mainly of surprise, but it was enough for her to slacken her hold on Linda for just a moment.

Linda quickly rolled her body away, and before Alison could respond, she scrambled to her feet and grabbed the pole. It turned out to be a deck broom and was light and flimsy, but Linda held it in front of her like a sword, ready to fight.

Alison was on her feet now. Her face was beetroot red, and strands of hair clung to it. The two women, panting and wheezing, circled each other on the small deck, like prizefighters in a boxing ring.

"You bi..." Alison spat and broke first, lunging at Linda, who brought the broom up sharply and shoved the bristles into Alison's face.

To Linda's satisfaction, Alison howled in pain and clutched at her face. When she pulled her hands away, Linda grinned to see trickles of blood mixing with smeared lipstick.

The smile was soon wiped off her face.

"Ladies, ladies, as much as this is entertaining, it's time to stop," drawled Gary Binns, who was now standing on the deck at the foot of the steps.

He was holding a handgun and pointing it straight at Linda.

"See what she did to me?" Alison screamed. "Kill her now."

"Babe, calm down," Gary soothed. "Go up to the wheelhouse and steer the boat. That's a good girl."

"Don't you 'good girl' me," Alison shot back. "She's scarred me, I'm sure. Kill her, Gary."

"Will you just please steer the boat," Gary said, a note of impatience creeping into his voice. "I'll handle this."

"Handle what?" Linda said. "You two are under arrest."

That made Alison and Gary both laugh.

That was okay. Linda was playing for time. She figured she only needed two minutes.

"What's funny? I know you killed Charles Harrington and abducted Agnes Crofton and Jewell Winslow. We have all the evidence we need to put you two away for life. Unless you want to cut a deal and tell us all about the Nautilus Circle."

Gary snorted, but Linda saw his hand tremble just a bit.

"Don't listen to her, babe," Alison said. "I know what she's doing; she's—m"

"Will you go and steer the damn boat?" Gary bellowed.

"Yes, go on," Linda said. "And while you're up there, fix your makeup. Your wrinkles are showing."

It was lame, but it worked. Alison started yelling, and Gary shouted back, but Linda wasn't listening.

"Three, two, one..." she shouted and pointed.

The Goodfellas, left on autopilot, was heading for a rock protruding from the ocean, marked with a red blinking light. Linda didn't know much about marine signage, but she was pretty sure that a blinking red light wasn't a good thing. The Goodfellas was on a straight course for the rock, and Linda was fairly sure the boat would give it a glancing blow on the port side. Or was it starboard? Linda could never remember. Another yacht approaching from the other direction was honking its horn, and Linda caught a glimpse of people on deck waving their arms frantically to warn of the impending crash.

Gary, finally noticing their collision course, forgot the gun and raced up the stairs, and Alison was frozen in horror.

"You have lipstick on your teeth," Linda taunted and then wished she'd paid more attention to what was happening with the boat.

Gary had managed to wrench the steering wheel hard to port (starboard?) and had also turned on the thrusters, which groaned into life and jerked the boat.

It was enough of a jolt to send Linda flying against the rails of the stern. Before her hands could grab onto anything to stop her momentum, Alison Binns was on her and grabbed Linda's feet, pushing upwards.

Not again, Linda thought as her body sailed over the rails and she hurtled towards the water. The last thing she saw was Alison Binns' face smeared with makeup, looking like the Joker from the Batman movies, laughing maniacally. Then Linda hit the ocean, and for a second, the cold water took her breath away. Luckily, Linda did not hit any rocks, but she plummeted deeper before her brain kicked into gear, and she realised she had to do something to save herself. She struggled to get her shoes off. Then she forced her arms out of her jacket.

Then she kicked and kicked, hoping that she would be clear of the Goodfella's propeller and that Gary Binns wouldn't decide to reverse over her.

As she got nearer the surface, the water was churning, and it frothed and bubbled around her. Her lungs were burning, and even though she could see light, her legs wouldn't work quickly enough.

She pushed her hand upwards, and it hit something solid. With one last push, her hand clasped around the object, and she was able to pull herself up until her head broke through the surface, and she was gasping to fill her lungs with air.

She realised that she was holding a life ring. Could Alison Binns have tried to save her? But no. As Linda pushed hair out of her eyes with one hand and trod water, she saw the stern of the Goodfellas growing smaller in the distance.

"Are you alright, love?" A voice called from above her, and Linda saw anxious faces looking down from the other yacht, which had been approaching from the other direction.

Chapter Forty-Eight

Linda pushed open the double doors and entered the foyer, carrying a grocery bag. All at once, she smelled antiseptic and cleaning fluid, the familiar odour of hospital waiting rooms.

She stopped briefly at the Shell Bay Hospital reception to ask for directions, and a stern-faced nurse pointed down a hallway, harshly illuminated by fluorescent strip lighting.

"Third door on the right," she said. "A private room."

Linda nodded her thanks and headed down the hallway. As she got nearer to the door, the smell of cleanliness was replaced by something else. Greasy food.

Typical, Linda thought.

Before knocking on the door and entering right away, Linda glanced through the glass window. Constable Ray Reynolds was sitting up in bed, his head bandaged and his arm in a plaster cast. According to Croud's updates, Ray had a nasty concussion. He'd lost a lot of blood from a horrible gash in his side from falling timber, but luckily, none of his major organs had been damaged. He had broken ribs and one arm, but the prognosis was good. Ray would make a full recovery.

Not only that, he would receive a commendation for bravery, for saving the lives of Agnes Crofton and Jewell Winslow.

After huddling together in the corner of the museum's basement, the two ladies had made it out without any major injuries, although Agnes had not stopped complaining about her rheumatism which was acting up after lying on a concrete floor, and Jewell would have a scar above her eye from the blow which Chad had dealt her.

Linda watched Ray as he dipped into a polystyrene carton of french fries, oblivious to the grease that dripped down his unshaven chin. Clearly, his appetite was unaffected by the trauma he'd suffered.

"Hello Ray," Linda said cheerily, as she stepped into his room. "How are you feeling?"

"Sarge." Ray beamed, dropping his french fries all over the bed. "You came to see me."

"Of course I did." Linda rolled her eyes. "I wanted to make sure you weren't faking it."

Ray laughed and then winced. "No, Sarge, I promise. But I'm getting better."

"I can see," Linda said, helping him clean up his fries.

"How are you doing?" Ray asked. "After your dip in the ocean?"

Linda laughed. "I'm fine, but I really have to stop doing that."

"What have you got there?" Ray asked eagerly, nodding towards the bag Linda had set down on the bedside table.

"Grapes," Linda answered, and Ray's face fell.

"Right, thanks Sarge," he said, but couldn't hide his disappointment.

"And six muffins." Linda grinned. "Natalie sent them. She didn't even charge me. They are her way of thanking you for saving her Aunt Agnes."

Ray coloured up, and mumbled, "She didn't have to do that."

Linda sat on an uncomfortable-looking plastic chair beside Ray's bed and looked directly at him.

"It was a very brave thing you did, Constable Ray Reynolds. The whole town is very proud of you. Even the mayor is planning a reception for you. As long as you don't mention that the whole incident was mostly his fault."

Ray managed a smile, but Linda could see his eyes glistening.

"I'm not a hero," he said in a shaky voice, "I... I had to rescue them. Because it wasn't the mayor's fault, Sarge. It was mine."

A tear rolled down his cheek and dripped onto the bedclothes.

"Why's that, Ray?" Linda asked softly, although she thought she knew the answer.

"Because it was me, Sarge," Ray burst out. "It was me all along. I was the one giving Shadowcaster all the information. And if I hadn't done it, then he wouldn't have known about the manuscript, and Agnes and Jewell would never..."

Linda nodded. It all fit. Every time there was a development in the case, Ray had been on his cell phone, and then there was Ray's shifty behaviour whenever the podcast was mentioned.

"Why did you talk to him, Ray?" Linda wasn't ready to let him off the hook yet.

Ray shrugged and winced again, clutching his ribs. "I dunno," he said. "I guess I enjoyed all the excitement. I've lived in Shell Bay all my life, and it's never been this exciting. I felt sorta down in the dumps after the Hiscock's murder was all over, and all the people were drifting away, and nobody wanted my autograph... so when I got the call fromShadowcaster, I just thought...."

He gave Linda a tired smile. "I knew it was wrong, Sarge. And I'm really sorry. But I didn't think it would do any harm, and then..."

"Ray, it wasn't your fault," Linda said, deciding Ray had suffered enough. "Yes, it was an idiotic thing to do, but it wasn't your information that caused Jewell and Agnes to be kidnapped."

"It wasn't?" Ray perked up a bit. "How did Binns know about it?"

"He, and whoever he works for, knew about the manuscript all along. They followed Charles Harrington to Shell Bay, knowing he was researching the death of his father and Douglas and Eliza Crofton. When they killed him and couldn't find the manuscript, they engaged Chad's services."

"But I thought Chad was talking to Shadowcaster too?"

"That's what Chad thought," Linda explained. "But we showed him a picture of Gary Binns' tattoos and he identified them as the same as the ones he'd caught a glimpse of, plus we found a voice distorter device on Binns' boat. So Chad was providing all the gaps in the information they needed."

"Right." Ray's shoulders sagged in relief. "What will happen to Chad?"

Linda shrugged. "If he testifies against Binns, then he'll get treated leniently, I should think."

Then she asked, "Do you have any idea who Shadowcaster really is? He's stopped broadcasting."

Ray shook his head. "I've been thinking about it, but I have no idea. I suppose anyone can do a podcast, right Sarge?"

"I suppose so. But a person would need to have equipment, wouldn't they?" Linda wondered out loud.

"Sure. A proper microphone and computer equipment. Plus all the right software to edit and produce it. Shadowcaster is a professional, not just some kid recording with a phone. He'd have all the up-to-date technical knowledge and some kind of sound studio."

Linda stared at him. The hairs on the back of her neck prickled and for a moment, she wasn't sure why. Then she put it together.

"Ray," she said, standing up. "You bloody deserve that commendation. And the podcast thing? If Croud pushes for an investigation into the leaks, I can't keep this to myself. You know that. But I will put in a good word for you, alright?"

"Thanks, Sarge. And sorry again. I won't be looking for any more excitement, I can tell you."

He smiled at Linda as she got ready to leave. "For a bit there, Sarge, I was just like you."

"Like me?" Linda was puzzled, "How were you like me?"

"I got addicted to murder, Sarge."

Chapter Forty-Nine.

The door to the Whispering Tides Bookstore jangled as Linda walked in.

The lights were on, and the neon sign in the window blinked *Open*, but there was nobody at the cashier's counter and no customers browsing the shelves.

Linda didn't call out. She stood for a moment to see if the doorbell roused any movement, but the whole store seemed still and deserted.

Linda strode past the rows of bookshelves until she came to the back of the store. There was one door, marked 'Private, Staff Only.'

Linda hesitated, wondering how to play it. Then, in a decisive move, she flung the door open.

Alex Harding was standing with his back to her, shaking his hips from side to side, and humming tunelessly under his breath as he took mugs out of a cupboard and placed them in a box.

"Alex," Linda said. There was no response. "Alex," Linda shouted, and this time, Alex swung round, startled.

"Oh my goodness," he said, removing small earplugs from his ears, "I didn't hear you. Listening to music." He held up his earphones. "Sorry, were you there long?"

"How on earth will you know if there are customers in the store?" Linda asked, ignoring his question.

Alex gave a small sigh. "To be honest, I'm not getting many customers." He smiled ruefully. "I think they preferred the store when it was a jumble, you know? Shell Bay readers liked sorting through piles of books. They don't really trust my recommendations or my labelled shelves."

Linda nodded. "Well, Shell Bay is a unique community," she agreed. "I did wonder why you chose to come here. Seems a strange choice for an entrepreneur."

The man's expression didn't change. He just shrugged. "I don't know. I guess I'm just attracted to quirky places."

"But I understand you are moving on," Linda continued. "I was down at the marina, and Fiona tells me you've given notice."

"That's right. This move hasn't worked out the way I thought it would." He smiled, and Linda thought again how good-looking he was.

"What will you do with the store?" she asked.

"The previous owner will take over as manager. She misses it more than she thought she would. So that all worked out."

"So you are packing up now?"

Linda took a long look around the small room. It was empty, except for a coffee maker on the counter and the mugs Alex was packing in the box.

"Won't take long," he said. "There's not much of my personal stuff here."

"What about in there?" Linda pointed to another door.

"Just a storage cupboard," Alex said. "Mostly empty."

Linda nodded, and then walked over to the door and opened it. It was dark, and she felt around for a light switch. This windowless room, too, was empty, except for two tables pushed together and a chair.

"Looks like you've really cleaned up," she said.

"Yes," he replied. "I'm just about done now."

For a moment, Alex Harding held her gaze. "Was there something you wanted, Detective Sergeant? Or is this just a social call?"

Again, Linda didn't answer him. Her eyes went to the earplug he'd placed on the counter. "Do you ever listen to podcasts?" she asked, watching his face for a reaction.

"Not really my thing," he answered quickly. Too quickly?

"So you haven't been listening to Shadowcaster?"

"Can't say I've heard of him," Alex said hesitantly.

"Shame. Shadowcaster has been broadcasting a series of episodes which he calls Death on the Dock. It's all about recent tragic events here in Shell Bay. They have been really popular."

"Have they?"

Linda continued, "Yes. True crime, as they call it, was never my thing either. I spend my whole day dealing with the aftermath of real-life crime and the horrible effects it has on people's lives, so I've never had any time for people who turn it into a form of entertainment. I don't know how they live with themselves."

Alex Harding was quiet for a minute. Then he said, "I imagine that these podcasters are fulfilling a demand. People all over the world listen to true crime podcasts and watch documentaries. I don't know why they do. Maybe their lives are dull and they need some excitement, but if nobody wanted to listen to them, they wouldn't exist. Just my opinion, Detective Sergeant. Now, if you don't mind, I am quite busy."

"I'll leave you to it," Linda said, and she turned and walked back through the store.

As Linda left the doorbell jangled behind her, she remembered what Ray had said as she left him at the hospital. Am I really addicted to murder? She thought about the excitement she felt every time a poor soul was found dead in suspicious circumstances. Was it just the thrill of the chase? Or was she as bad as the true crime podcasters and their macabre shows, and the audiences who greedily consumed them?

Linda suddenly felt very tired. She checked her phone. It was the end of the day, and all the paperwork at the office could wait until tomorrow. She thought of the bottle of red wine she'd left for Agnes to find underneath her sink and smiled. Time to go home and have a drink with the old bat.

Chapter Fifty

Linda Jenkins leaned back in her chair, stretched her arms up, and yawned loudly.

There was nobody to hear her. It was Saturday morning. Wenda didn't work weekends, nor did Croud. Constable Ray Reynolds had been out of the hospital for three weeks and had come back to work part-time, but decided to take some vacation. He and his family were going to the mainland, he'd told Linda, with a pleased look on his face.

"What are you doing over there? Visiting Granville Island? Having a walk around Gastown?" Linda guessed.

"No," Ray had said, sounding surprised. "We're going to IKEA."

Linda decided not to question Ray any further. If they wanted to spend three days wandering around IKEA, it had nothing to do with her. Ray had been through a lot lately.

He managed to stay humble, even though he had been the recipient of many free coffees and muffins, and Croud had officially nominated him for a bravery award.

Croud had dropped the investigation into the podcast leaks, so Linda had not seen any reason to reveal that it was Ray who had been giving information to Shadowcaster. After all, Ray's instincts about Chad Garner and Gary Binns had been spot on. Linda had to give him that. So Ray deserved his break, and if Swedish department stores were his thing, she hoped he enjoyed every minute of it.

Linda had come in on her day off to work through a pile of paperwork. It was essential that all the I's were dotted and the T's crossed because Gary and Alison Binns had employed some exceedingly expensive lawyers, who had already managed to arrange bail for the couple while awaiting trial. The coastguard had stopped the Goodfella barely half an hour after Linda had plunged into the water. As Linda had hoped, Fiona had alerted them.

The Binns had claimed they acted in self-defense after Linda trespassed on their boat and attacked them.

In the weeks ahead, Crown Counsel had warned Staff Sergeant Croud to expect delaying motions to be filed, which may keep the Binns out of the courtroom for months, even years.

The case file had to be complete and perfect.

So Linda had taken advantage of a quiet Saturday morning to go through it all once more, just in case.

Sadly, there was no smoking gun that linked the Binns to Charles Harrington's murder—quite literally. A thorough search of their boat and penthouse in Vancouver hadn't turned up any firearms at all. There was no direct evidence to link them to the abduction of Agnes Crofton and Jewell Winslow either.

Gary Binns had just shrugged when Linda questioned him about the demolition of the museum.

"We get calls like that all the time," he said. "I don't know who it was. Good job we didn't do it because we would never have got paid. Whoever called us used a fake number. Probably a prank." He'd grinned and spread his hands. "Kids these days, eh?"

There was no trace of the mysterious man who'd visited the mayor, and no grant money ever arrived in the city's bank account.

Linda tried without fail to trace Shirley Grimm, who had left the country to retire 'somewhere warm'. She had found out from the delivery company that they had been paid to pick up the envelope from Victoria Airport and deliver it directly to Linda's home.

Unfortunately, because the photographs of the skull and the bullethole could not be verified, they would not be admitted into evidence. And because the crime scene technicians insisted that the skull did not exist, the only evidence that Charles Harrington's death was a murder was the grainy footage from the marina.

The only useful testimony they had against Gary Binns was a written statement from Chad Garner. Chad and his lawyer had negotiated a plea deal for the assault of Agnes and Jewell in exchange for his testimony against Gary Binns. Chad would testify that it was Binns who had ordered him to destroy the footage. Luckily, Chad was smart enough to figure out that the footage might be useful as leverage in the future and had kept a copy. It wasn't much, but Linda hoped it would be enough to put the Binns behind bars for a long time.

Linda shuffled the papers into a neat pile and placed them in a file. As she bent down to drop it into the desk drawer, she caught sight of the box under her desk. She had kept copies of all the documents Natalie had given her and a copy of the manuscript.

The original was locked in a safe, ready for the court case.

Linda doubted the manuscript would be useful evidence. Although it was an engrossing story, written in Charles Harrington's loopy cursive, it read like a true crime conspiracy theory, something Shadowcaster would broadcast, all speculation and little factual evidence.

The Nautilus Circle. Did this organisation really exist? And if they did, were they as sinister as Charles Harrington believed? Were they really responsible for Eliza and Douglas Crofton's deaths, and did they have power and influence over politicians and the top brass in the police force? And even if they were guilty of all those things, what on earth could Linda Jenkins, a lowly Detective Sergeant, do about it?

With a sigh, Linda closed the desk drawer and stood up. The Nautilus Circle was a problem for another day. She'd promised to have lunch with Agnes.

As Linda picked up her jacket and walked towards reception, she heard the entrance door creak.

"Hello?" she called out. "The Detachment is closed. If you need police assistance, you'll have to..." Her voice trailed off as she reached the foyer and found a man standing there, an amused expression on his face.

"My dear, I don't need police assistance. I just need to have a chat with you."

Linda Jenkins sat across from the man, who was impeccably dressed. There was nothing out of the ordinary about him, except his expression, which could best be described as cold, amused arrogance. He sat upright and crossed his legs.

Linda leaned back in her chair, trying to seem relaxed, although there was something about this man that made her feel uneasy.

"Ah, Detective Sergeant Jenkins." His lip curled upwards in an imitation of a smile, although it didn't reach his eyes. "Congratulations on the con-clusion of your latest investigation. However, despite all your hard work, I'm afraid that Mr and Mrs Binns, objectionable and vulgar as they are, are unlikely to face a prison sentence. The whole case will be dismissed."

Linda kept her voice level. "I don't think so. I don't know who you are, but if you are part of Binns' swanky legal team, one call to the judge will get you disbarred. Threatening a police officer..."

The man laughed and spread his hands wide as if to show he had nothing to hide.

"My dear, I'm not threatening you at all. I am merely informing you of what will happen next. The Binns will go free, Harrington's death will be recorded as a tragic accident, and eventually, Ms Crofton and Ms Winslow will recover from that unfortunate prank."

"Prank? They nearly died. And Gary Binns held a gun to my head and tossed me in the ocean. That is against the law. He'll go down for that and for everything else. Unless he tells us who he works for, that is." Linda glared at the man. "Maybe it's you? Who are you?"

The man ignored her question.

"Detective Sergeant Linda Jenkins, once Detective Inspector Jenkins of the Major Crimes Unit, disgraced because of an administrative error, was it? You got an address wrong and let a drug ring go free? Or were you demoted because of an ill-advised liaison with a married detective? Jared, I think his name is. Handsome man. Good police officer too. Does what he is told, I hear."

Linda couldn't help letting out a small gasp. "How do you know—"

The man held up his hand to stop her talking. "There isn't anything I don't know about you, Detective Sergeant."

He reached into his jacket pocket and withdrew a small, embossed card, holding it up for her to see. On its surface, the Nautilus Circle logo gleamed in the dim light of the interrogation room.

"Do you know what this represents, Detective Sergeant?" he asked, his tone almost mocking. "This is more than just a simple logo. It's a symbol of power, of influence that extends far beyond your limited understanding of the world."

He traced a finger over the stylised nautilus shell at the centre of the logo, his eyes never leaving Linda's face. "The nautilus, you see, is a creature of the depths. It navigates the darkest waters with ease, adapting to the pressures that would crush lesser beings. And that, my dear Detective Sergeant, is what the Nautilus Circle embodies. We are the ones who chart the course through the shadows, who wield the secrets that shape the very fabric of society."

His smile widened, becoming almost predatory. "The twelve stars? They represent the chosen few, the inner circle of our organisation. Each one a guiding light in the darkness, a master of their own domain. And the Latin phrase, 'In Profundis Sapientia'? It's more than just a motto. It's a promise. In the depths of secrecy, we find the wisdom to control the world above."

He leaned forward, his eyes boring into Linda's with an intensity that sent a chill down her spine. "You see, Detective Sergeant Jenkins, the Nautilus Circle is not some petty gang of criminals for you to hunt down and bring to justice. We are the ones who make the rules, who pull the strings from behind the scenes. The law, as you so quaintly put it, is a tool for us to use, not a constraint to be bound by."

He tossed the card onto the table between them, the logo staring up at Linda like a mocking challenge. "The Nautilus Circle is not just a symbol, Detective Sergeant. It's a reminder of the futility of your efforts. You may think you're fighting for justice, but in the end, you're just a tiny fish swimming in a vast, dark ocean. And we? We are the ones who control the tides."

With that, he stood, straightening his jacket with a nonchalant tug. "Now, if you'll excuse me, I have more important matters to attend to. Good luck with your paperwork, Detective Sergeant Jenkins. Don't work too hard."

Epilogue

Joseph surveyed his kitchen at the back of the Dine on the Dock restaurant. He was tired but satisfied with his work. He'd completely re-vamped the menu, and tonight was the perfect time to test out his new recipes.

It was a special occasion. Jewell and Agnes had been saved. Linda and Ray were heroes, and another murder had been solved. But apart from that, Joseph had some exciting news to share with his friends.

Joseph left the kitchen and went into the restaurant. He fiddled with the napkins and cutlery and inspected the floor for dust. He wanted everything to be perfect. Nothing could go wrong tonight, he was sure of it.

Agnes and Linda walked down the ramp to the dock. It was early evening and dark, but Sea Breeze Marina was lit up with lights strung along the docks, illuminating the way to Dine on the Dock restaurant.

Agnes had grumbled all the way because Linda had not allowed her to smoke in her car. Now, Agnes was complaining about the way the docks were rocking as the tide came in.

"It's not safe," she huffed. "Why would anyone eat in a floating restaurant? It's already making me queasy." She shot a look at Linda. "I'm not eating any crab," she said, "not since..."

"Alright, alright," Linda sighed. "There'll be something else on the menu, I'm sure. You'll enjoy it. I promise. It's a special occasion. Joseph has opened the restaurant just for us."

Agnes pursed her thin lips and nodded. "I'll just have a cigarette before I go in," she said when they got to the restaurant door.

Linda stood with her as Agnes lit up, and the familiar plume of smoke circled in the cool evening air.

The bruising on Agnes' face had faded, and the cuts around her wrists, where she had been bound, had healed. There were almost no physical signs of the older lady's ordeal. But Agnes had lost her spark. She no longer hovered outside Linda's window, and she wasn't standing waiting for Linda to pepper her with questions at the end of every shift. She hadn't even snooped around Linda's apartment, even though Linda had dropped heavy hints about bottles of wine hidden in the cupboard under her sink. Linda missed the old Agnes. She hoped that an outing with other people whom Agnes could insult would encourage a return of her feistiness.

It had been a week since Linda's meeting with the nameless man. It was odd, she thought. Even with her police training and observation skills, she hadn't been able to put together a reasonable eyewitness description of him. All she'd come up with was 'white male, between thirty and forty years of age, average height and weight, and brown hair and grey eyes'. Or was it grey hair and blue eyes?

If it wasn't for the shiver of foreboding every time Linda thought about his warning, and his amusement as he shared details of her life and career that were supposed to be in a confidential personnel file, Linda might have believed she imagined the whole meeting. But then there was the tangible evidence: the business card with nothing on it except a logo. The same logo tattooed on Gary Binns' arm. The logo of the Nautilus Circle.

In the last week, Linda had submitted her files to the Crown Prosecution. Ray had checked in on Chad Garner and reported that the lad was nervous and had lost his bravado, but was doing well. Croud had got a pat on the back for keeping within budget and had splurged on an order of Mocha Choca Crunch muffins, which Natalie had actually delivered.

"Don't get used to it," she snapped as she left the box on the desk in reception, but Linda noticed that there were two extra muffins included with the order.

Linda had eyed the boxes under her desk and thought about pulling them out and sorting through the contents, but so far, she hadn't done so. Agnes and Natalie had waited for justice for years, she thought. Another week wouldn't make much difference.

"Hi there," a voice said, interrupting Linda's thoughts, and she looked up to see Fiona Driver locking her office door.

"Hi," Linda said. "How are things?"

"Oh, fine," Fiona replied. "The marina is quiet at this time of year, which is good, because I don't have Chad working at the moment. Only Justin. He's slow but getting better. He's just finishing off for the day, and I'm off home too. You're having dinner at the restaurant tonight?"

Linda nodded. "Yes, with Sarah and Jewell. And Ray," she added.

"That's good. I hope you get some closure for Jewell," Fiona added. "She's been lost these last weeks. It's very hard," she said, "when you don't know the whole truth. It's one thing to know who killed Charles, but why? What possible motive would that terrible man have to kill Charles?"

"I don't know," Linda said with a pang of guilt, visualising the boxes under her desk. "I'll work on it." And she meant it.

"You do that, Detective Sergeant," Fiona said. "Enjoy your meal. Good-night."

Agnes finished smoking, ground her cigarette butt out, and put it in a trash can after Linda had glared at her when she went to toss the butt in the water.

Then Linda pushed the restaurant door open and waved at Sarah, Jewell, and Ray, who were sitting at a table with large glasses of red wine in front of them.

They all looked happy at least, Linda thought. Jewell looked pale and drawn, but she nodded and curled her lips up as Linda and Agnes walked over to the table.

"Wine, Sarge?" Ray asked as Linda and Agnes sat down.

"No, she won't," Agnes said as she settled into her seat. "She's driving. But you can pour me one, young man."

Ray dutifully filled a glass and put it in front of Agnes.

Linda filled a glass full of water from a jug on the table and looked around.

"Here we all are again," she declared and raised a glass. "Here's to the Wharf Rats of Sea Breeze Marina."

"Oh, I'll drink to that," Sarah said, and even Jewell looked happier and raised her glass.

Joseph appeared from the kitchen. "Hang on," he said. "You can't have a toast without me," he declared, so they did it again.

"Right then," Joseph said. "Who is ready to order?"

"I know what I'm not having," Agnes said, twisting her thin lips into a smirk, and Linda glared at her again.

Agnes waved her hand, and turned to Joseph. "What's wrong with you?" she demanded. "You look as excited as a puppy rolling in sh—"

"I have something to tell you all," Joseph interrupted. "But dinner first. I want to know what you think of my new menu."

As Joseph stood by the table, his pencil poised over a notebook, ready to take orders, the door to the restaurant swung open. They all looked around to see Justin stumble into the restaurant.

His hair was wilder than usual, but as he pushed it back from his forehead with a trembling hand, Linda could see his pale face and large terrified eyes.

"You all... you all gotta help me..." he gasped, and Linda got up and rushed over to him. She got there in time to grab the boy before he collapsed to his knees.

"What's the matter?" Linda asked urgently, standing over him. "Justin, why do you need help? What's happened?"

Justin looked up, tears streaming down his face.

"There's... there's a body," he finally managed to get out in a hoarse voice. "There's a body in the boathouse..."

The End.

Also by Jackie Sharp

The Wharf Rats Mystery Series

Murder At The Marina

Body in The Boathouse

The Carroll and Delaney Mystery Series

A Secret War

The Victory Murder (2025)